Lucky Dog

and Other Tales of Murder

Lucky Dog

and Other Tales of Murder

Dick Lochte

Five Star
Unity, Maine

Five Star First Edition Mystery Series.
Published in 2000 in conjunction with Tekno Books and Ed Gorman.

Cover design by Brad Fitzpatrick.

Set in 11 pt. Plantin by Anne Bradeen.

Printed in the United States on permanent paper.

Library of Congress Cataloging-in-Publication Data

Lochte, Dick.
    Lucky dog and other tales of murder / by Dick Lochte.
        p. cm. — (Five Star first edition mystery series)
    Contents: Lucky dog — Rappin' dog — Sad-eyed blonde — Vampire dreams — A tough case to figure — Get the message — Murder at Mardi Gras — A murder of import — Mad dog.
    ISBN 0-7862-2688-9 (hc : alk. paper)
    1. Detective and mystery stories, American. I. Title. II. Series.
PS3562.O217 L83 2000
813'.54—dc21   00-034753

Table of Contents

Introduction   7

Lucky Dog   13

Rappin' Dog   49

Sad-Eyed Blonde   73

Vampire Dreams   97

A Tough Case to Figure   113

Get the Message   121

Murder at Mardi Gras   143

A Murder of Import   165

Mad Dog   175

Introduction

Why do you write detective stories?

That's usually the second question people ask. The first is: what made you become a writer? I have no real answer to that one. Mental imbalance? Goofy chromosome? Lousy at math? For whatever reason, I started writing stories when I was in grammar school (elementary school they'd call it now) in New Orleans. I've no idea what those tales were about, though I suspect the OZ books by L. Frank Baum, which I was into at the time, might have been a major inspiration. In fourth grade, I broke into print when the local newspaper, *The Times-Picayune*, ran my contest-winning essay about Richard Wagner's *The Flying Dutchman*. I hadn't heard one note of the opera, but I didn't let that stop me from writing three hundred words on the subject. An early example of the new journalism.

My introduction to mystery fiction took place in my early teens, when I picked up a book of my mother's, *The Second Saint Omnibus*, a collection of short stories and novellas by Leslie Charteris featuring the modern Robin Hood. Not long thereafter, at the home of a friend, I spotted a book his brother had just finished, a Pocket paperback edition of Raymond Chandler's *The Big Sleep*. The cover had Philip Marlowe (looking remarkably like a scowling Gregory Peck) discovering the voluptuous Carmen Sternwood sitting on an ornate chair, stoned to the gills and naked as a grape.

Chandler joined Charteris on my growing mystery shelf. A few Ellery Queen titles snuck in there, along with the odd Mr. and Mrs. North. I discovered Craig Rice's great screwball comedy capers featuring John J. Malone, attorney, and his fast-living pals, Jake and Helene Justus. Frank Gruber's raffish pair, Johnny Fletcher and Sam Cragg, drifted in and Nero Wolfe added his considerable weight.

Although I was reading very little else for pleasure, it didn't occur to me to try to write a mystery until I was in college and wound up working part-time for a detective agency in New Orleans. The owner of the agency, known as Elmo for purposes of this introduction, was a very dapper gent—homburg, yellow suede gloves, walking stick. The works.

Considering that the main thrust of the agency's business was down-and-dirty repossessions, the style of dress may have been a little over the top. But Elmo was politically connected, which, in Louisiana, is the same as saying he could wear whatever the hell he pleased as long as he didn't embarrass the governor.

He was actually a pretty good guy. And he didn't make me do any repo work, for which I was grateful, being kind of skittish about sneaking prized possessions away from angry (and armed) folks who were down-on-their-luck. Elmo hired me to behave like a college student. That is, he wanted me to visit his clients' establishments, usually in the French Quarter.

I'd sit at the bar, sip a few cocktails and try not to get too drunk, while surreptitiously observing what the bartender did with the cash.

It may seem like an easy gig, but not when you're a naïve student who's never had to nurse a drink before, much less deal with aggressive, thieving B-girls and attractive hookers and feisty bartenders who really didn't want their bosses finding out that they were neglecting to ring up every third sale.

I hit the bars once or twice a week for several months. Some nights, I'd be assigned other duties, like sitting in parked cars in residential neighborhoods, trying to stay awake while observing houses and apartment buildings and making notes on who went in and who came out. Unlike most of the detectives I was reading about, Elmo had absolutely no scruples about doing divorce work.

And so it went—a different sort of education than the one I was getting on campus, but as it turned out, an education nonetheless.

I sold my first short fiction, "Medford & Son," to *Ellery Queen's Mystery Magazine*. It was a tale about a very 1960s generation gap (a little too dated for this collection, I think) with an O. Henry-type twist at the end. Nearly twenty years passed before I wrote my second short story.

In between, I graduated, worked at a local television station, edited the Southern edition of a national magazine, sold tours to Europe and Asia, wrote advertising and promotion copy for *Playboy* in Chicago. I spent more than a decade in Southern California as a film critic for the *L.A. Free Press*, a theater critic for *Los Angeles* magazine and a book columnist for *The Los Angeles Times*. Finally, in 1985, I published my first novel, *Sleeping Dog*, which introduced a new detective team—world-weary, middle-aged private eye Leo Bloodworth and precocious, TV-addicted teenager Serendipity Dahlquist. The book, consisting of dueling first person narrations by both Leo and Serendipity, was well-received and was nominated for an Edgar and just about every other prize in the mystery field. It won The Nero Wolfe Award.

I'd published two books in the series when Kathy Daniels, then editor-in-chief of *The Armchair Detective*, asked me to contribute a story, preferably with Serendipity and Leo. The result is "Lucky Dog," a tale involving them with members of the literary community, narrated by Serendipity.

She also narrates "Rappin' Dog," the most recent entry in this collection, which appeared in the anthology, *Murder on Route 66*, edited by Carolyn Wheat. This one has a vaguely musical background, which gave me the opportunity of calling attention to the talents of the late great songwriter and singer-musician Bobby Troup. It also has the distinction of being loosely based on an actual incident involving an extortion attempt on a television personality.

"Sad-Eyed Blonde" originally appeared in the anthology *Raymond Chandler's Philip Marlowe*, edited by Byron Preiss. A number of authors were asked to write "new" stories about Chandler's famous private eye. My favorite Chandler novelette is "Goldfish," so I wrote a sequel and I thought it might be amusing to toss a little Hammett into the mix. According to contract, my use of the "Philip Marlowe" name is limited to the anthology. I was going to substitute another name, when I realized I'd only used a couple of "Phil"s in the original. Now the detective narrator has no name, but I doubt anybody will confuse him with Bill Pronzini's famous sleuth "Nameless."

Preiss next asked me to submit a short for his anthology, *The Ultimate Dracula*. What he got was "Vampire Dreams," a semi-supernatural who-done-it. I had plans to use the vampire sleuth again, but never got around to it. Now, thanks to the television series "Angel," the idea isn't so original any more.

For the Serendipity-Leo novel *Laughing Dog*, I created a secondary character—a New Orleans detective named

Terry Manion—who went on to become the protagonist of two novels based in my native town, *Blue Bayou* and *The Neon Smile*. "A Tough Case To Figure," which was written for *Ellery Queen's Mystery Magazine*, contains a rather roundabout reference to the Bloodworth-Manion association.

"Get The Message," which began life in a journal published by Southwestern Louisiana University, is the only short story to feature Terry Manion.

In 1996, David Talbot, the founder, chairman and editor-in-chief of *Salon*, asked if I wanted to create a short who-done-it for a weekly contest that the Internet magazine had launched. Readers were being challenged to e-mail their solutions to the mysteries, with gift certificates for books offered as the rewards for their winning efforts.

In the prologue to the novel *Blue Bayou*, Terry Manion's mentor, a seasoned private eye named J.J. Legendre, was murdered. But he refuses to stay buried. He is the hero of the first half of *The Neon Smile*, the part of that novel that takes place in the 1960s when he was alive and well and a member of the New Orleans Police Department. Marilyn Stasio, in the *New York Times Book Review*, said he walked away with the novel.

For the *Salon* short, I decided to resurrect J.J. once again. "Murder at Mardi Gras" occurs in the late Sixties, when the detective has quit the NOPD to become the chief investigator for district attorney James Garrison. "Mardi Gras" and "A Murder of Import" (both considerably reworked for this collection) were among five Legendre stories that have appeared in *Salon*.

"Mad Dog," featuring Leo Bloodworth without Serendipity, originated in *Santa Clues*, a collection of Christmas crime stories edited by Martin H. Greenberg and Carol-

Lynn Rossel Waugh. It is loosely based on events in the colorful life of Winnie Ruth Judd, the so-called Tiger Woman, who, after being convicted of a gruesome double murder, escaped several times from various institutions and was eventually paroled. I was particularly pleased with the way the story turned out, which may be why, in my own perverse way, I've saved it for last.

Dick Lochte
Palm Springs, California
April 8, 2000

Lucky Dog

On that smoggy July 9th afternoon of my fifteenth summer I was sitting at a borrowed desk in a tiny room that was part of the Leo G. Bloodworth Detective Agency, staring rather forlornly at my computer monitor. The only sentence on it, "Hello, Serendipity Dahlquist, welcome to the wonderful world of words," was supposed to make me feel as though the machine was conversing with me. But as I'd been staring at that same message from my supposedly user-friendly software for nearly an hour, the effect was rather underwhelming.

It wasn't the computer's fault. It was doing its job. I was the one who had not the heart nor the concentration to give it words to process.

I was a published author, thanks to two previous books based on actual experiences I'd shared with Mr. Bloodworth. Initially, I had come to the highly recommended detective for help in finding a beloved dog that had been spirited away. Upon completion of the difficult and perilous search that ensued, I wrote a personal account of its often terrifying and, for me, quite painful events. Great minds thinking alike, Mr. Bloodworth penned his own version. As fate would have it, his publishing house was absorbed by mine and the two works were combined in a single volume, *Sleeping Dog*.

Shortly thereafter, the intrepid sleuth and I had another adventure. Once again, we were surprised to find ourselves "collaborators," on a book titled *Laughing Dog*. Since both works were reasonably well-received, our publisher encouraged us to continue to work in tandem, and I was perfectly satisfied to spend a few more years, at least until I was twenty-one, compiling other books with the well-known sleuth. But Mr. Bloodworth, being of that unenlightened generation that still considers a teenager a child, or perhaps merely wishing to be beholden to no other person, man, woman or young adult, decided to end the literary partnership. He was gracious enough, however, to allow me the office space to pursue my muse, solo.

That day, my muse was apparently as distracted as I about the news of Missy Lambert's untimely death. "The forty-year-old, best-selling novelist whose romans a clef prompted fear and loathing on both coasts, died here in Los Angeles yesterday of causes yet to be determined," the round headed anchorman on Channel 8 had read breathlessly.

Since I'd never met Ms. Lambert, I did not exactly burst out in tears. And I certainly would not mourn the loss of any future barely-fictionalized character assassinations that she might have written. And yet I grieved for her passing for a personal reason: she and Mr. Bloodworth had just begun some sort of relationship.

I had proceeded no further with my word processing when I heard the outer door to the office creak open and close. I recognized the detective's heavy footsteps. I imagined him entering his office, removing his jacket and sitting down at his scarred and battered desk, running his thick fingers through his thin sandy-colored hair.

At the sound of his squeaking chair, I got up and strolled over to visit. He was slumped at his desk, looking as gloomy and pathetic as a contestant who'd just muffed the "Final Jeopardy" question. I knocked on the jamb and his big head lifted from his chest and his striking yellow eyes stared at me. "Hi, kid," he said. "No school today?"

"It's summer vacation, Mr. B.," I informed him. "I've been spending my days here for over a month. You may remember the nice talk we had last Monday."

"Oh, right," he said, rather listlessly. He did not look well. His usually ruddy complexion was as pale as paste, except for a dirty golden stubble on his chin. His suit was as rumpled as if he'd slept on the beach at Bay City and been caught in high tide. "The last twenty-four hours have been a real bear," he said, reading my thoughts. "Not much sleep."

"The Lambert woman's death was on the news this morning," I told him. "There was a clip of you ignoring a reporter. Everybody seemed to ignore the reporter. I tried phoning you."

"I've been . . . out."

It was possible that he was drunk. Or perhaps hung over. I took a few steps backward to the ancient coffee-maker and poured a cup for him. His heavy eyes opened a few millimeters as he sniffed it, then drank it. He winced and grumbled, "The worst goddamned sludge I've ever tasted."

"You're welcome," I said, frostily.

"I'm sorry, kid. I'm past the polite stage." He exhaled. "It looks like Missy killed herself."

"Oh." I could sense his pain, but I didn't know what else to say.

He placed the nearly full cup carefully on his desk. "I wish I could come up with something else to call it, but I was there in her apartment and I saw what happened."

"What did?" I asked. "If you feel you can talk about it."

He waved a hand in hopeless resignation. "We were having a conversation. She excused herself and went into her bathroom. I sat there like a bozo watching the dust settle for nearly twenty minutes before I figured something was wrong and busted the door in."

15

"The door was locked?"

He paused, then nodded. "I guess it was. Yeah. Anyway, when the lock splintered, that brought the maid and the dog-walker on the run. We went in and found her." The memory of it pushed him further into the chair. "She was lying on the carpet, with only a spark left. I used CPR, but by the time the paramedics showed, she was a goner. She'd gulped down a whole bottle of sleeping pills."

I frowned. "Unfortunately, when people live by drugs, they sometimes die by drugs."

Mr. Bloodworth sighed, and his face took on that exasperated look it gets when I've disappointed him. "I'm sorry," I told him. "I try not to be judgmental, but it's just my way."

"Don't believe everything you read, kid. That stuff about Missy being an open-all-night swinger was just publicity hogwash. She sold a lot of books by pretending she was as wild as any of her characters. Fact is, she took pretty good care of herself. The only thing she drank was soda with little lime slices. And I've never seen her eat anything that wasn't fit for rabbits."

"But she obviously used sleeping pills. What brand, by the way?"

He cocked his head and said, "They're not sure. There was no label on the empty bottle. The M.E.'ll figure it out by the time of the inquest, I guess."

"Inquest?" I asked. "Does that mean the police aren't certain it was suicide?"

"Inquests are part of the package when celebrities fade out like this," he said. "Even if Missy hadn't been a favorite of the talk shows, it's sorta unusual for suicides to take themselves off with people waiting around for them. Unless they don't really mean to go through with it." His face contracted in excruciating mental anguish. "Jeeze, maybe she was expecting

16

me to stop her. Maybe that's why she waited until I got there."

"Wasn't she acting weird or anything?"

"Well, she was . . . I don't know, sort of dreamy, I guess. Maybe even slurring."

"But you said she didn't drink."

"She didn't. This was more like when you get up in the morning and your tongue isn't working right."

"My tongue's always working," I said, hoping a little self-deprecation would lighten his mood. When it didn't, I went on, "Maybe she'd just awakened. Even the earliest riser sleeps in every now and then."

"Nope. She told me she'd had a meeting early that morning with her agent. She'd been up for hours."

"I suppose she might have had some sort of medical problem," I said. "Some nerve or muscle thing. That could have been the cause of her depression."

"But she wasn't depressed. She seemed on top of the goddamn world. I keep telling myself it was an accident."

"But if she was about to have lunch with you why would she even take one sleeping pill by mistake, much less enough to do her in?"

"I'm familiar with the question," he said hopelessly. He slumped even lower, his chin pressing into his yellow and red striped tie. "Guess I'll head over to the Irish Mist and try to change the subject."

"You've spent enough time at that low den," I snapped back. "You should go home and rest. You look terrible."

"I can't sleep. I keep running that half hour through my mind, wondering if I missed a chance to head her off."

"How long had you known her?" I asked him.

"A week. But it's been a long week."

"Still, after just a week, do you think she would have

counted on your picking up on her mood and taking away her pills?"

"She told me she thought we were secret sharers."

"Oh, please," I said. "Secret sharers, really."

He looked at his watch. "Yep, I think I'll hit the old Mist. Happy Hour in forty minutes."

I started to protest, but he was already on his feet and heading out the door. I went back to my unfinished novel.

I didn't see him again for several days. Not even in the footage of Missy Lambert's funeral which ran on every newscast. Four prospective clients called the agency and I dutifully relayed the information to his home answering machine, but I had no idea if he were working or moping or worse.

Then, one typically tepid, hazy afternoon, he strolled in and, would wonders never cease, entered my tiny workspace and plopped down in the empty chair. He looked at the page of type on my monitor and asked, "New book?"

"I thought I'd write about the Halliwell case," I told him. It had been a rather tricky industrial espionage thing in which I'd assisted by using my computer to access a company's coded files.

"Make sure you change the names and the basic situation," he said.

"I've done that," I said, studying his face. It had regained its usual ruddy color. He looked considerably more rested than he had at our last meeting. But he was still depressed.

"It's official," he told me. "Missy died by her own hand. Case closed."

"You've been at the inquest, huh?"

"The star," he said. "The star of the inquest."

"So it's suicide," I said.

"What else could it be? According to the M.E., she'd

probably taken a bunch of pills even before I got to her apartment. That's why she was slurring and moving so slowly."

"They ever find out the kind of pill?" I asked.

"Dalapams. The fastest-acting of all the sleeping pills. The M.E. says it's possible she was so out of it she may not have known she was gobbling a fatal dose."

"Then it could have been an accident," I said brightly.

"Yeah," he replied. "Except for the suicide note."

"Oh. Then I guess she wasn't quite the happy, healthy woman you thought."

Mr. B. grew gloomier than ever. "It sure looks that way. In any event, she's gone. So long, Missy."

"You really cared for her, huh?"

"Hell, I was just getting to know her," he said. "Or not know her, as it turns out."

"How'd you two meet?"

Mr. Bloodworth scowled. "What's the difference, now?"

"If it's some sort of secret, I understand. Us not being secret sharers."

He looked away. He was hiding something. He made a few "harumph" noises and said, "I bumped into her at a shindig and we sort of hit it off."

"What type of shindig?"

"A dinner party this guy invited me to."

"What guy?"

"Her, ah, publisher. Armand Dieter."

His sheepishness suddenly made sense. Apparently Mr. Bloodworth was befriending a new publisher, Mr. Armand Dieter, to make sure that our writing "partnership" would cease.

"Interesting," I exclaimed.

"What's interesting?"

"Armand Dieter. He's rather the wunderkind of publisher's row. Came out of nowhere to become the late Marcus Dane's heir apparent and successor at the helm of Dane & Dunlop. Dashing, flamboyant and outspoken about his work and his authors, but fiercely protective of his private life. He has homes in New York, London, Paris, Los Angeles and some ski place. Switzerland, I think."

Mr. Bloodworth scowled. "How do you know so much about him, sis?"

"He was profiled a few months ago in an issue of *Vanity Fair* magazine. He was on the cover, riding on the back of an elephant in Kenya, or somewhere. Was the party business or pleasure?"

"Uh, pleasure, I guess," Mr. Bloodworth said. "Anyway, I found myself sitting next to Missy at dinner."

"Freud says there are no chance happenings."

"Yeah, well, he might have changed his mind if he'd been at this dinner. Anyway, we met and, like I say, we hit it off."

"What'd you two talk about?" I asked. "During dinner, I mean?"

"This and that."

"Her work?"

"She wouldn't get into any of her new projects. Superstitious. But she said she'd read my . . . *our* books and liked 'em. She wanted to know how our manuscripts happened to get combined, like that."

"Mainly book talk, then?" I asked.

He nodded. "I suppose. She also wanted to know a little about criminology."

"Oh?"

"How'd I get in the business? Did detectives operate differently in L.A. than they did in New York? Did I know an investigator named Henry Longo in Manhattan?"

"Do you?"

He shook his head, "No."

I swung my feet onto my desk. Mr. Bloodworth frowned at my purple gym shoes, yellow ankle socks, and rolled jeans. Before he could begin to lecture me on the need for more sedate attire around the office, I asked him to tell me exactly what transpired at Missy Lambert's apartment the day she died.

"I just went through it all at the inquest, but I guess once more wouldn't hurt."

He described arriving at Ms. Lambert's apartment building, the Wilshire Arms, at noon that fatal Wednesday. The maid, Juanita, a Salvadoran he thought, led him through a spacious apartment with a living room "roughly the size of Burbank," to a den at the rear "with a wet bar, a writing desk, a couple sofas, pop art crap on the walls and French doors opening onto a large balcony overlooking the West Side as far as the Ocean.

"Missy joined me in the den, looking great as usual. Only, as I said, her reflexes were off a little and her tongue was sticking to the roof of her mouth. She made me a martini and herself an O.J. She was upbeat, smiling. Not a bit depressed."

I frowned. "What'd you talk about?"

"Uh, the weather, the view. Then her pooch wandered in, followed by this dog-walker, Felix."

"What kind of dog?"

"His name is Swifty. Off-white hair sticking straight out and thin little legs. Looked like a cross between a powder puff and a rat, but a kind of endearing little critter. Just like you, kid." He paused, waiting for a retort.

"If that's the case, I'm surprised he didn't nip you on the ankle," I told him. "What's this Felix like?"

"Tall, pale, one of those bluebeard guys who always needs

a shave. Maybe twenty-five. Skinny as blue milk. The dog got along with him, but my feeling was that he was more interested in something around the apartment other than the pooch."

"Could he have been Missy's lover?"

Mr. Bloodworth shrugged. "I wouldn't have thought so, but I haven't been much of a second guesser where she was concerned."

"How long was Felix with you both in the room?"

"Ten minutes, tops. He and Missy discussed the flea problem. Swifty has this allergy to the little bloodsuckers that makes him scratch like crazy even when he's not carrying. Then Felix headed back to the kitchen. And Missy went through her bedroom, into her bath and overdosed on the Dalapams."

"Felix did nothing to upset her?"

"Not that I saw."

"He didn't pass her the pills, or anything like that?"

Mr. Bloodworth thought a moment, then shook his head "no."

"Could you be more precise about the events once Felix left you?" I asked.

Mr. Bloodworth shut his eyes. "The dog hopped onto the couch beside Missy and she picked it up and stared into its eyes. She said something about cataracts and . . ."

"Whoa. What about cataracts?"

Mr. Bloodworth's eyelids lifted, disclosing his peculiar golden irises. He scowled. "She had to feed the dog cortisone pills to give him relief from the allergy. And the pills have been known to cause cataracts in animals. I mumbled something like, 'You'd think that medical science could come up with a pill with no after-effects.' And she winked, shooed the dog away and stood up."

" 'That reminds me . . .' she said. And with that, she excused herself and did the deed. 'That reminds me.' I reminded her to take the damn pills."

"And the suicide note was found in the bathroom with her?" I asked.

"Nope. On a table in the room she used as an office. Addressed to Dieter."

"Written when?"

"They're not sure. Maybe the same day. Probably before she started swilling the pills, because her handwriting was steady."

It was all very confusing and, worse yet, illogical. "Whom did she see at that early meeting?" I asked.

"Her agent, a guy named Jericho."

"Maybe he said or did something to throw her into a depression. But if that's the case, why didn't she take the pills then? Why'd she wait for you?"

Mr. Bloodworth stared at the carpet.

"Did you see the suicide note?" I asked.

"Yeah. I must've read it over five or six times."

"You remember what it said, exactly?"

He shut his eyes again and squinted, as if using his memory caused his head to ache. " 'Dearest Armand, I'm sorry. It will be painful for you, I know. We have been such good friends as well as business associates. But I must do this. I wish I could explain. But when my inner voice speaks, I must obey. Try not to think too badly of me . . .' Pretty much like that. Signed, 'Missy.' "

I hopped from the chair. "Do you think you could get us into her apartment?" I asked.

"Why?" he wanted to know.

"Because unless we look into this, you may continue moping for the rest of your life. And I won't have that."

"Yes?" the maid, Juanita, inquired, eyeing us suspiciously from the doorway.

"I'm Leo Bloodworth. I was here when Miss Lambert . . . passed away."

"Yes?"

"I seem to have lost something and I think I must have left it in the den."

"Yes?"

"A cigarette lighter. There's an anchor on it and an engraved battleship . . ."

"Yes?"

"Why don't we just come in and see if it's there?"

"No."

"Excuse me," I said to the maid. "Is there a reason you're wearing a bathrobe at three in the afternoon?"

Mr. Bloodworth suddenly realized that the woman was, indeed, dressed in a bathrobe. "Takin' a snooze?" he asked.

She looked at us, totally confused.

"Who's that, Juanita?" a male voice demanded from a room to the left of the door.

She replied something in Spanish and a pale man appeared behind her. He was barefoot, dressed only in black cotton pants and a sleeveless undershirt. In his arms was a little yipping dog, a toy, white with brown mask and ears. A papillon. Rather rare. I'd seen pictures of the breed before, but never an actual animal. He looked both angry and frightened. Rather like the pale man.

"Hi, Felix," Mr. Bloodworth said, pushing past Juanita. "Having a dog day afternoon?"

Felix looked from Mr. Bloodworth to me and back. "What do you want? Our instructions are to allow no one in here."

"As I was just telling Juanita, I think I left my lighter in the den. Don't let us disturb you," Mr. Bloodworth said, moving forward. "You two and the mutt can go back to your grieving, or whatever, and we'll hunt around for the lighter."

I stepped through the front door just as Felix placed a hand on Mr. Bloodworth's chest. The little papillon stopped yipping and began to bark in earnest. "You are not supposed to be here," the pale man said without much conviction.

"And you are?"

"I have been caring for Swifty." He looked at the gown-clad housekeeper and added, "I am also comforting Juanita."

"Comfort on, then," Mr. Bloodworth said, brushing past them.

"Please," Felix almost shouted. "Do not make me call the police again."

Mr. Bloodworth paused. "Again? Why'd you call 'em before?"

"Because of the crazy man who came the day after the Madame passed away. He threw Juanita to the ground and ran into Madame's office. He also attacked me. I did not know what to do. I called the police."

"Who was he?" I asked.

"I don't know. He left before the police arrived."

"What did he look like?"

"Tall," Felix said. "Thin. Fine features. Almost pretty. Black hair gathered at the back of his head in a tail."

"How old?" I asked.

"Perhaps thirty," Felix said. "He kept repeating, 'It isn't here,' over and over as he ran away. I think he was maybe on drugs."

"What'd the cops tell you?" Mr. B. asked.

"When I explained that the man took nothing from the apartment, they appeared to lose interest. Though they made a report. I am . . . uncomfortable around police. But if you

25

force me, I will summon them again."

"No need for that," Bloodworth told him. "We'll be out of here before you know it."

"Sir?" Felix asked.

Mr. Bloodworth stared at him.

Felix seemed to shrink a little. "Is it possible," he wondered, "for you and your daughter to take Swifty when you go?"

"She's not my daughter," Mr. Bloodworth said. "And before you start deciding the mutt's fate, you'd better wait and see what Madame Lambert's will has to say."

Felix's voice shook slightly. "Swifty is not mentioned in the will."

"Who told you that?" I asked.

"Mr. Loup, her lawyer, was here this morning with the will's executive."

"That's 'executor,' " I corrected him.

"Execu-tor, then. Since Juanita is mentioned, but does not speak English so good, they informed me of the contents of the will."

"How much did Juanita get?" Mr. Bloodworth asked.

"She was left comfortably, as they say. But it is Madame Lambert's brother who is to inherit the bulk of the estate, nearly seven million dollars."

Mr. Bloodworth gave him a nod signifying he was impressed by the amount. "I don't suppose any of the estate had your name on it."

"No," Felix replied quickly. "Nor did I expect that. Especially when I learned that poor Swifty was not himself mentioned. The lawyer said that Miss Lambert's brother wishes for the dear canine to be turned over to the animal shelter. A creature so pure bred, sharing a small cage with mongrels. So sad."

"It is that," I agreed. "Are you sure you can't take him?"

"As much as I love him, I cannot afford his care."

"Maybe Juanita would like to split her inheritance with the dog," Mr. Bloodworth mumbled cynically as he walked toward the rear of the apartment.

"Poor little Swifty," Felix crooned, petting the animal's tiny head and calming it a bit.

"I have my own dog," I told Felix. "Otherwise, I might consider giving Swifty a home." It was not really the truth. Swifty wasn't a particularly friendly animal. When he began to bark again, I went off to find Mr. B.

He was in Missy Lambert's office. It was pale violet with gray trim. One long wall was filled with books, my idea of heaven. There was an off-white, ultra-plush wall-to-wall carpet and over it a subdued Oriental rug that stopped just short of a modern, glass-enclosed fireplace. An antique desk sat against a wall under a picture window that looked out on a northern view of Westwood Village. On the desk was a powerful little laptop computer. Mr. Bloodworth pointed out a space next to the computer. "That's where they found the suicide note."

The space was now empty and spotless. Missy apparently had been a neat person. Beside the laptop was a printer with a very small footprint and separating the two machines was a sleek, black, halogen lamp. A telephone and an answering machine were also on the desktop. Nothing else.

In the center desk drawer was a box of sharpened red pencils, a plastic dish with paper clips, a stapler, a tape dispenser and a silver letter opener from Tiffany's with the initials MGL.

The side drawers contained indexed files. I flicked through them. There was one file guide, labeled *Smile of the Wolf*, that was empty. I wondered if the man who broke in was referring to the *Wolf* file when he said that "it" was not there.

I told Mr. Bloodworth about the missing file. "Doesn't *Smile of the Wolf* sound like a book title?"

He agreed that it did. He glanced at the files and shrugged. "Maybe the agent has it."

I opened the laptop and turned it on. There was a series of electronic bleeps. Then a message read, "Insert Diskette." A bad sign, indicating that the hard disk was not functioning. Wiped clean by someone? I turned the machine off, and replaced the lid.

Then I moved on to the wall of books and studied their spines. For a woman who wrote such junk, she certainly read the right stuff. Daphne DuMaurier, George Sand, Dorothy L. Sayers, Edith Wharton, Virginia Woolf. And, quelle surprise! One shelf over was a title authored by a male. I plucked that volume and began to leaf through it.

Mr. Bloodworth grumbled, "I hope we didn't come over here just so you could shake the dust off her books?"

"Looking at someone's library is tantamount to listening in on their therapy session," I told him.

"Oh?" He sounded dubious.

"This one, for example. It's by Mr. Aldous Huxley." I perused its dust jacket. "*After Many A Summer Dies the Swan*. It seems to be about a fellow searching for eternal life."

"Eternal middle age. Now there's a scary thought," he said. "What's it tell you about Missy?"

"I don't know, yet," I said, studying spines as I replaced the Huxley. Missy kept most of her fiction in one area. The Huxley was mixed in with an assortment of books with titles like *Forever Plus One*, *Beat Aging By Beating Bacteria*, *The Body Preserved*. I said, "Actually, it seems that your friend was most intrigued by the notion of longevity."

"Sure," he said sarcastically. "That's why she killed herself."

Was he being purposely obtuse? I suggested that he look at the books. He ambled over and hunkered down, fingering a few of the volumes.

"And those," I said, pointing to a lower shelf. He recited the titles down there. "*The Prince of Publisher's Row, My Random Years, Bestsellers By the Dozens, My Pal, Max Perkins, Dinner with Alfred, My First Fifty Editors.*" He gave me a bored look. "So?" he asked, creakily rising.

His deductive capabilities had definitely gone on the big sleep along with Missy. I said, "So nothing. I'd like to see the bathroom now."

Ten minutes later I had convinced myself that no one but Missy Lambert could have administered the fatal drug dose. I said, "I assume the police removed the empty pill bottle. Did you see it?"

"It was brown. Plastic, I guess. With a white cap. Like I said, no label. I gotta tell you, sis, you're getting very good at this business."

I explained, "There's a wonderful little manual that is available from the Treasury Department, 'Crime Scene and Evidence Collection Handbook.' I'd be glad to lend you my copy."

"Thanks," he said with some irony.

I opened the medicine cabinet. "There are no drugs in here whatsoever. But she seems to have been an excellent customer of the Great Health store. Just look at the megavitamins and minerals." I shifted a bottle of Chewable Papaya with Enzymes and discovered the only genuine medicine in the cabinet—a barely-used bottle of cough syrup prescribed by a Dr. Nagle.

Suddenly, a perplexed voice from the doorway said, "What the devil's going on here?"

The man was rather handsome. In his thirties, tall and

thin, dressed in a loose silk shirt, jodhpurs and riding boots of the kind preferred by film directors in Hollywood's golden era. He'd been wearing that same sort of outfit on the cover of *Vanity Fair*.

"Oh," Mr. Bloodworth said, smiling at the jodhpurs. "Hiya, Dieter. Leave your horse with the doorman?"

"I was getting ready for polo, Bloodworth, when Felix called to say you had forced your way in here."

Felix and Juanita were standing just behind the man. Felix was cradling little Swifty in his arms.

"We didn't mean to upset anybody," I said.

The publisher gave me a glance. "Ah, this would be your writing partner, Miss Dahlquist?"

Mr. Bloodworth nodded imperceptibly. He asked, "Why'd they call you, Dieter? You the keeper of the keys?"

"Merely the executor of Missy's estate," Mr. Dieter said. "But I really don't understand what you're doing here, going through poor Missy's things."

"I, uh, left my lighter last week."

"In the bath?"

"Perhaps we'd better go," I said.

Mr. Dieter nodded to Mr. Bloodworth. "We had an incident here right after Missy's death. Fellow broke in and—"

"Felix told us," Mr. B. interjected.

"Well, then, you can understand why we want the rooms closed until an inventory can be made. If we come across your lighter, I'll make sure you get it."

He accompanied us from the apartment. In the elevator, I asked, "Mr. Dieter, what's *Smile of the Wolf*?"

He raised an eyebrow. "I'll bite. An Ingmar Bergman movie?"

Mr. Bloodworth said, "A file with that title is missing from Missy's desk. Know anything about it?"

"*Smile of the Wolf?* It's very catchy. Maybe even kitschy. No, I've never heard of it. The files, and everything else, belong to her brother, Jamie. I suppose he could have taken your *Wolf* file for some reason."

"Aren't you curious about it?" I asked him. "You being her publisher and all?"

The elevator door opened and he moved through it. Mr. Bloodworth, ever the gentleman, waited until I had exited. Mr. Dieter paused at the front door and said, "I'm not sure why Missy gave her file that title, but I'm fairly certain it wasn't the name of a book of hers. Missy confided in me that she hadn't written a word in nearly two years. She'd dried up. Perhaps that was at the bottom of her despair."

"Still," I maintained, "the file could contain notes or an outline."

Dieter smiled genially. "We can always hope, can't we?" He pivoted on his boot heel and moved quickly past an obsequious doorman. His Jaguar convertible was parked directly in front along the curved driveway. He got in, gave us one final wave and roared away.

"What a strange man," I said. "I'm not sure I'd want him for my publisher."

Mr. Bloodworth sighed wistfully and said, "Well, kid, why don't we pack it in?"

I stared at him. "Suppose Missy was murdered?"

"You know she wasn't."

"But let's suppose she was, and the police, thinking it was suicide, refused to investigate. What would your next move be?"

"I'd go talk to some people—the lawyer, Missy's agent."

"Let's do it," I told him.

"Why? She wasn't murdered."

"Because, at the very least we may discover that the reason

31

she took her life had nothing whatsoever to do with you."

He blinked and then nodded. "Beats washing my socks," he said.

Attorney Abel Loup was a tanned, fit specimen in his early forties, wrapped in an immaculate conservative dark gray suit. He greeted us cordially in the antique-furnished waiting room of Marx, Loup, Lefcourt & Stern and escorted us to his splendid, equally antique-y office in the corner of one of the few reasonably well-tended old buildings in downtown Los Angeles.

There was a pudgy, pale man in his thirties seated on Mr. Loup's couch, scowling at us. He was balding prematurely and had a variety of nervous mannerisms from an eye tic to an annoying sniffle to a frequent baring of his teeth in a grimace. Though he, too, was dressed in a conservative suit, I knew immediately that he was not one of Mr. Loup's associates. If there were any fat lawyers, which I doubted, it would be highly unlikely that you would find them in Southern California, at a firm as prestigious as Marx, Loup.

He was, as Mr. Loup's introduction informed us, James Lambert, Missy's brother and heir. "Since you said you had something to tell me about Missy's will, Mr. Bloodworth, I thought Jamie should be present also."

James Lambert stared at us and his face broke into an inappropriate grimace. We'd decided that Mr. B. would ask the questions since not everyone takes me seriously until they get to know me.

"How long ago did Missy make her will?" he inquired of lawyer Loup.

"Why do you ask?"

"I was wondering if it could have been as long as a few years ago. Before she got her dog."

The lawyer paused, then replied, "It was a recent will. A very recent will, in fact, dated the week before her death. I was rather surprised to learn of its existence." He turned to James Lambert.

"I was equally surprised," the heir said in a nervous, nasal voice, sniffling and grimacing. "Missy didn't like to think about death. Our parents passed away in an automobile accident when we were very young. Missy refused to attend their funeral and pretended that they were 'away on a trip.' Now she's taken a trip herself." A very inappropriate bare-tooth grimace.

"If you didn't put the will together for her," Mr. Bloodworth asked the lawyer, "who did?"

"It appears to be a simple will generated by a computer program that Missy prepared herself. Ever since I became her lawyer, I tried to get her to make out a will, but she always brushed away my concerns. I suppose she bought the software when she decided to take her own life. The will was found among her effects."

"By whom?" Mr. Bloodworth asked.

Mr. Loup looked at Mr. Lambert, who shrugged. "By the police, I suppose," Mr. Loup said.

"Why'd she make Armand Dieter the executor, Mr. Loup? Why not you?"

"I don't know. I can't tell you why Missy did any of the things she did recently."

"You're sure the will's legitimate?" Mr. Bloodworth asked.

"What's that supposed to mean?" Mr. Lambert shrieked, his face turning blotchy.

"The signature is unquestionably hers," Mr. Loup said quickly. "I did run it past an expert. And we are abiding by the will, unless," he indicated me, "your client feels she has just reason to contest it."

Lawyer Loup had leapt to the wrong conclusion that I was the client. I stopped Mr. Bloodworth from clarifying the situation. "I was merely wondering about Swifty," I said. "Couldn't a small portion of Miss Lambert's estate be set aside to care for the animal properly?"

Mr. Loup looked at me, puzzled. Mr. Lambert squeaked, "The dog? Damnit, Loup, you got me down here to talk about a mangy mongrel?"

"I . . . perhaps I misunderstood the reason Mr. Bloodworth gave for this meeting."

Mr. Bloodworth shot me a look that said, "Time to go."

"The animal is not mangy," I said. "And he is definitely not a mongrel. He is a most unique breed."

Mr. Bloodworth grabbed my arm and moved me toward the door. "Sorry to have bothered you, gentlemen," he said. "Let's keep in touch."

As we walked to the parking lot for Mr. Bloodworth's car, I said, "Your secret sharer's brother is a neurotic worm."

"A wealthy neurotic worm," he added.

"With a nervous grin that very much resembles a 'smile of the wolf,' " I said. "I wished I could have asked him about that missing file."

"You can phone him when I'm not around," Mr. Bloodworth replied. "I personally never want to see that geek again. Or the lawyer."

"On to Missy's agent, then," I said with a cheerfulness I did not feel.

"I've used up my embarrassment quota for the day, kid."

"But I've arranged this one better," I said. "I didn't have to lie to get us in."

He looked at me and sighed.

The Creative Career Management building in Beverly

Hills was a four-story granite structure that was austere enough to have served as the headquarters for a union. Martin Jericho, the president of CCM, was thought by some, himself included, to be one of the most powerful men in the entertainment industry. But he apparently had not forgotten his early days in the business when he'd assisted my agent, Lacey Dubin. One phone call from her and he agreed to donate a few minutes of his precious time to Mr. Bloodworth and myself.

He was a tiny, round man in a thousand-dollar suit with a head of long wavy blond hair that looked as if it belonged on a wrestler. He ushered us into his creamy-white oval office. After offering us coffee or tea, scones and brownies so rich I could feel my face break out just for smelling them, he asked what he could do for us.

"We were wondering what the reason was for your meeting with Missy on the morning she died," Mr. Bloodworth asked.

Martin Jericho's eyes hooded and he made a steeple out of his fingers. "Why do you want to know?"

"I was with her when she took the pills," Mr. Bloodworth explained. "I've been trying to figure out why she did it. I thought maybe your meeting—"

"Let me interrupt you right here," Martin Jericho said. "Nothing transpired at my meeting that could have caused her to do such a thing. She seemed happy and healthy. She wanted to talk about a new book she was working on."

"*Smile of the Wolf*," I said.

"Huh?"

"Wasn't that the title of the new book?" I asked.

"Beats me," he said. "Missy wouldn't tell me a thing about it. Except that she wanted me to market it at some house other than Armand Dieter's. I was surprised, since I knew

35

Armand had pushed her onto the bestseller lists and they were very close."

"Didn't they have a contract?" I asked.

He shook his head. "No, indeed. If one of my clients hits the top of the bestseller lists, that client signs no multiple-book contracts. Dieter was automatically given first bid and the opportunity for a final bid. And he'd published all of her books. But not this new one. She was closing him out."

"Why?" Mr. B. asked.

"I don't have the foggiest. Missy said that it wasn't personal; they were still very good friends. The last I saw of her, she and Armand were hugging."

"Dieter was with her the morning she took her life?" Mr. Bloodworth asked.

"Yeah. He showed just as our meeting was breaking up. Why?"

"It didn't come up at the inquest."

The agent shrugged. I mentioned what Mr. Dieter had said about Ms. Lambert drying up and being unable to write. Martin Jericho frowned. "Unkind. And untrue. Of course, I didn't actually see the manuscript, and authors do get into trouble . . ."

"Did Missy ever lie to you before?" Mr. Bloodworth asked.

"No, but . . ."

"Maybe the new novel was about one of those live longer clinics," Mr. Bloodworth added, trying to jog something loose from the agent's memory.

"What gave you that idea?" Martin Jericho asked.

Mr. Bloodworth told him about the books in Missy's library. I was pleased to see his deductive processes were in working order after all. The superagent grinned. "I guess you didn't know Missy that well, huh, Bloodworth? She was sort of, um, eccentric when it came to, um, health care. One week she'd be talking about essential oils extracted from flowers, the next it was past life therapy. Acupuncture, hypnosis, yoga, polarity therapy, colonics. She's been through 'em all. She was a tough cookie about everything else, but when it came to gimmicks for hanging onto your youth, she was the easiest mark in town. Four or five years ago, she even had this shaman she wined, dined and clothed for months until I found out the guy was an out-of-work actor, about as Native American as Sylvester Stallone. My point, Leo, is that the subject of longevity was too dear to her heart for her to play around with it in one of her novels."

"But if she was so interested in living, why did she commit suicide?" I asked.

"Sweetheart," Martin Jericho addressed me, immediately erasing whatever respect I might have had for him, "if I knew the answer to that, I'd think I was even more brilliant than I really am."

"Was she easy to do business with?" I asked.

His face froze. "Easy? Honey, if writers were easy to do business with, my two daughters would know me a little better than they do. Missy was . . . demanding. But not unfairly so."

"Did she have any enemies?"

He grinned. "Every time a book of hers arrived on the bestseller lists, another writer's book went off. Enemies. Then there were the people who thought she was writing about them. And the people who knew she was writing about them. Every novel shook somebody's cage hard. And she only went after the big boys and girls. But what could they do? Fiction is fiction."

"This crook who was conning her," Mr. Bloodworth said, "was he a tall guy, pretty-handsome?"

"Black hair pulled back into a dork knob?" I added.

"A what?" Martin Jericho asked.

"A little ponytail," I explained.

The superagent nodded, running a hand over his own immaculate mane. "That's about right."

"Remember his name?" Mr. B. asked.

"Never forget a name. Killburn. Mark Killburn." He smiled proudly.

"Any idea how we could find him?"

The agent's smile grew wider. A telephone appeared in his hand as if by magic. "He's an actor. Of course I know how to find him."

Forty minutes later we were in room 412 of the Sea Esta Apartments in Venice watching Mark Killburn pace up and down around an unmade Murphy bed. The walls of the studio apartment were mottled by salty ocean moisture and the carpet was pitted with sand. I was standing next to a window rather than risk sitting on a stuffed chair that looked as though it were hosting a convention of mites. Mr. Bloodworth sat on the bed.

Mark Killburn, wrapped in billowy black trousers and black and white striped shirt, had just told us that he had never heard of Missy Lambert.

Mr. Bloodworth reached out, grabbed the man's ear and twisted it.

Things had gotten off on the wrong footing the moment the man answered the buzzer. He was angry and abusive, and he used a rather rude epithet to describe me, which dissipated Mr. Bloodworth's geniality to the point where he grabbed the fellow by his striped shirt and sort of dragged him back into his apartment, tossing him onto the stuffed chair.

Mark Killburn admitted that it had been he who had broken

into Missy Lambert's apartment on the day after her death.

"Why?" Mr. Bloodworth asked him.

That was when Mark Killburn hopped to his feet and began to pace. He tried to borrow a cigarette from Mr. Bloodworth. The detective said, "We didn't come here to be your pal, Killburn. We just want to know why you broke into Missy's apartment."

"I did some work for her and she didn't meet the price we agreed on."

"So, since she was dead, you were gonna steal enough to get even?"

"Look, pal. I wasn't going to steal anything. She owed me."

"What'd you do for her?"

Mark Killburn waved his hand airily. "I took a trip, did a few things, got some information for a book she was writing."

"Could you be a little more specific?" Mr. Bloodworth demanded.

Mark Killburn shook his head. "I don't think so. I don't do anything without getting paid for it." He grinned.

Mr. Bloodworth gritted his teeth. I couldn't tell what was on his mind, only that it might get him in trouble. Before he could lay hands on Mark Killburn again, I said to the loathsome pretty boy, "Did Miss Lambert send you to New York?"

The man glared at me, but he didn't deny it.

"And did you work with a man named Henry Longo?"

Mr. Bloodworth was starting to smile now, remembering the name.

When Mark Killburn said nothing, I went on. "Then suppose I tell you approximately the job Missy Lambert hired you to perform."

And I did.

Later, as Mr. Bloodworth and I were driving back to the office, he said, "All this information is very interesting. We've got the motive for murder, but the problem is there was no murder. Missy killed herself."

"She was obsessed by longevity," I said. "She was working on a book. She met with her agent to discuss the book. She invited you to lunch. Hardly the profile of a suicide."

"But I was there," he said heavily. "She took the pills."

"I know," I told him. "But that doesn't mean she killed herself."

The next day, while the morning sun burned-off the remaining dew from the grass on the polo field in Will Rogers State Park, Armand Dieter turned his pony over to a handler. He then walked from the field, carrying his white helmet and mallet. He was dressed in a sweat-soaked striped rugby shirt, white jodhpurs and high leather boots. He placed his gear on the convertible's passenger seat. Then he turned and saw us—Mr. Bloodworth and me, and our good friend, Lieutenant Rudy Cugat, of the Bay City Police Department, resplendent in an elegantly cut pale green suit.

Mr. Bloodworth said, "You looked good out there, Dieter. Good form."

The publisher stared from him to Lieutenant Cugat.

Mr. Bloodworth introduced them. Neither man made any attempt to shake hands.

Mr. Dieter said, "If you'll excuse me, I must be going. I'm headed back to Manhattan this afternoon."

"I doubt it," I said.

"What?"

"I don't think you're going anywhere until you explain why you gave Missy Lambert the pills that she used to take her life."

The publisher mumbled something under his breath and began to get into his car.

"Señor Dieter," Lieutenant Cugat said. "We would like you to explain about the pills."

Dieter stared at him. "What sort of nonsense is this?"

"Do you know a Doctor Roy Nagle?" Mr. Bloodworth asked.

Dieter answered, "I don't believe so. Did he claim I gave Missy any pills?"

"No. He was Missy's M.D. Internist. Whatever. Anyway, he never prescribed any Dalapam for her. Never pills of any kind. Doctor Nagle says she was afraid of 'em. Thought they slowed down the body's clock."

"So?"

"So, where did the fatal pills come from? And how did they get into her O.J.?"

"Why ask me?" Mr. Dieter said, edging back toward his car.

"Do you know a Doctor Weismann?" I asked the publisher.

His head whipped around in my direction. "What about Weismann?"

"He's your doctor, isn't he, Dieter?" Mr. Bloodworth asked.

"My internist in New York. Yes. But how did you . . ."

"Your secretary told us," I offered.

"She's usually more discreet."

"It's not her fault," Mr. Bloodworth said. "Somehow she got the idea that you'd eaten a bad clam and asked me to get in touch with your doctor, pronto.

"And don't go blaming Doc Weismann, either. He's a very ethical gent, by the way. I told him that I was a pharmacist out

41

here in L.A. and was about to refill your Dalapam prescription. But I wanted to check with him first. And you know what Weismann said?"

Mr. Dieter did not answer.

"The doc said he wanted you to call him before he would approve my giving you more pills. Said he felt that the Dalapam he prescribed just two weeks ago should have been enough to hold you for a while."

Dieter leaned against the car and folded his arms. He said, "Lieutenant Cugat, am I to understand that these absurd charades of Mr. Bloodworth's involving people in my employ, which may be considered malicious persecution, are the basis for your being here?"

"Well . . ." Lieutenant Cugat began.

"There's the suicide note," I said.

The publisher glared at me.

"Why would Missy have written a suicide note to you?" Mr. Bloodworth asked, forcing Mr. Dieter to switch his focus, get a bit off-balance. "You weren't her lover or a relative. You weren't even going to be the publisher of her next book."

"That was just a question of money," he said. "She was trying to get me to up my advance."

"Then you lied to us when you said she hadn't been working on a new book," I accused.

"It was none of your business," he said.

"Maybe Missy wrote that note as an apology because she was going to switch publishers."

"What is it, Bloodworth?" Mr. Dieter asked. "Is it because I decided not to offer you a contract for your childish dribble? Is that why you're hounding me?"

"No," Mr. Bloodworth said evenly. "Though you seemed to like my childish dribble well enough to invite me to dinner at your place. But that's not why I'm hounding you. It's because you killed Missy."

Mr. Dieter gave us a very convincing exasperated look. "She was changing publishers, so I killed her?" he asked scornfully.

"No," I said. "You killed her because she had to change publishers."

Mr. Dieter frowned at me, but I knew I had his full attention.

"The book she was planning was to be another of her infamous sex-and-scandal romans a clef, but the hero of this one was going to be a famous, outspoken editor-publisher, the sort who'd appear on the covers of smart magazines. The sort who'd romance his boss' wife so he could get her to intercede for him with her husband. And, later, to use her voting stock to make him head of the company."

"What absurd—?"

"Missy hired a sleazeball gigolo who calls himself an actor to go to New York and, well, get close to Oscar Dane's widow. A New York private eye named Henry Longo taped their conversations. Mrs. Dane talks a lot. Missy's book was going to be really something."

"This is the most ridiculous—"

"I spoke to Longo long-distance just an hour ago," Mr. Bloodworth said. "He sent tapes to Missy, but he kept a set."

"I don't know what you're talking about."

"We've got the gigolo's statement, too," I told him. "He was planning on blackmailing you. He broke into Missy's home the day after she died, trying to find her notes. But you'd already taken them."

"Absolute fantasy," Mr. Dieter said, hanging tough. But he was perspiring even more than he had from his polo match. He said, "What an imaginative child you are."

43

"It doesn't take much imagination," I told him. "Missy's library was filled with research books about the literary life. The letter addressed to you, as Mr. Bloodworth has pointed out, reads less like a suicide note than a request that you forgive her for betraying your confidences. Sometimes authors have no control over the compulsions that force them to write."

"You people are insane," Mr. Dieter sputtered.

"Then there's Missy's will," Mr. Bloodworth said. "The one making you executor of her estate. Her lawyer was surprised that such a document existed. Still, Missy's signature was authentic."

"Surprise, surprise," Dieter said sarcastically.

"But," Mr. Bloodworth replied, "it might be that Missy's signature was copied from another document, an old book contract for example."

"This is the kind of fantasy you should put in your books, Bloodworth. Why in God's name would I forge a will that doesn't put one penny into my bank account?"

"It did make you executor of her estate, putting you in control of her files just long enough to destroy the new novel and her notes," I told him.

Dieter shook his head. "Where is all this headed? What are you accusing me of? Missy took her own life. Missy wrote her own will."

"She definitely didn't do that," I said. "If she had, she would have included arrangements for her little dog, Swifty. She may even have made him sole heir, or something. She loved the dog, pampered him. She wouldn't have forgotten to see that he was cared for."

For the first time there was a hint of panic in Mr. Dieter's eyes. "This is . . . nonsense. The . . . woman . . . took . . . her . . . own . . . life."

"Yes," I said. "But it was you who got her to do it."

"I wasn't anywhere near her when she died," he almost shouted.

"You didn't have to be. You programmed her, just as I program my computer. When you arrived at her apartment that morning, you dropped several pills into her orange juice and made sure she'd had a glass. Then, lulled by the narcotic, she was more susceptible to phase two of your scheme. You presented her the Dalapams in an unmarked bottle. You told her that she should take a handful, just before lunch, which would give you all the time you needed to be far, far away.

"But before you left her apartment, you placed the letter she'd sent you about the novel on her desk. You realized it was vague enough to pass for a suicide note. But there were no pens on her office desk. The pens are on the writing desk in her den. Why would she write the note at one desk and then take it into another room to be found?"

Mr. Dieter seemed breathless now. "So she swallowed those pills, simply because I told her to. If I were that convincing, I wouldn't be standing here now, confronted by paranoids."

"Ms. Lambert was very open to alternative health care, no matter how unorthodox," I said. "I think you told her those sleeping pills were some sort of magic new product that would make her feel better or live longer. 'Take as many as you want,' I bet you told her. 'The bigger the dose, the faster they start working.' But instead of extending her life, the magic pills ended it."

Mr. Dieter's lip curled and he reached over the side of his Jaguar and grabbed his polo mallet. He swung it in an arc, barely missing my head.

Mr. Bloodworth growled, "Give it up, Dieter. You've done enough damage."

The publisher ran toward Mr. Bloodworth, swinging his

45

mallet wildly. Mr. Bloodworth took several steps backward, tripped and fell to the ground. Mr. Dieter loomed over him and raised the mallet.

"No!" Lieutenant Cugat shouted. He was pointing his police special at the publisher. Still, Mr. Dieter refused to give up. He hurled his mallet at the lieutenant who dodged it gracefully. Then Mr. Dieter turned and ran.

We followed as far as the edge of the polo grounds and watched him leap upon the back of a nearby horse and gallop away.

"Aren't you going to stop him?" I asked the lieutenant excitedly.

"Stop him? You want him to run. It's the best proof of his guilt." He turned to Mr. Bloodworth. "That's some shaky 'evidence' you assembled. The word of a gigolo. A New York detective's tapes of a woman's bedroom chat. I'm your amigo and I was more than happy to throw a scare into that snake. But I am grateful I did not have to push the limits of my authority past the point of no return by telling him I was arresting him for murder."

"You can see he's guilty," I said.

Lieutenant Cugat shrugged. "He attacked us with a deadly weapon. Then he ran. So there is reason to have him detained from leaving on a plane to New York. Past that, it will depend upon the deviousness of the District Attorney's office to build a case for murder."

"How devious are they?" I asked.

The lieutenant smiled. "Considering that Dieter purchased the pills that killed the woman and probably forged her will, I'd say they could throw a pretty good scare into him."

As we walked to the lieutenant's car, I asked Mr. Bloodworth, "If Missy Lambert's will is declared a forgery, is there a chance little Swifty might inherit some of her estate?"

"Gee, I don't think so, kid. The loot'll probably still go to her only living relative, brother James."

I frowned. "That hardly seems fair. She obviously would have wanted the dog to be cared for. Perhaps James Lambert might be talked into putting aside a small portion of his inheritance for Swifty."

"I wouldn't count on that," Mr. B. replied.

I flopped onto the back seat of the automobile and scrunched up my face in concentration. "There must be a way of getting him to change his mind," I said.

Lieutenant Cugat said to Mr. Bloodworth, "Amigo, I have a feeling that James Lambert will soon discover that being an heir has its drawbacks. Our Miss Serendipity will not be denied. With her looking out for his welfare, this Swifty is one lucky dog."

Mr. Bloodworth turned his head to face me. He winked and to my delight said, "That makes two of us."

Rappin' Dog

"Go to school,
"And play the fool,
"You get no help in the cruel world.
"Play it smart, get a fast start,
"There's an art
"To livin' large in the cool world."

The words of rapper B.A. "Big Apple" Dawg reverberated through the unmarked police van. I turned to Mr. Leo Bloodworth, the renowned private investigator, who was sitting next to me and said, "You're playing the fool when you go to school? That's the dumbest advice I've ever heard. The man's a cretin."

"You're preaching to the choir, Sara," he said, using his own clever diminution of my given name Serendipity.

The three LAPD detectives in the van, members of an elite team known as The Star Squad, were busy with their surveillance. The leader, a Detective Gundersen, asked, "You getting a good level, Mumms?"

"Just like stereo," Officer Mumms replied. She was a very cool black woman, seated at a table that had been bolted to the floor of the van, studying the various indicators on a tape recorder secured to the table.

"Wire's workin' fine," Detective Gundersen said to our driver. "Give Doggie Boy a honk."

The driver, Detective Lucas, tapped the van's horn twice.

He was a rather handsome man with more than a passing resemblance to Mr. John Kennedy, except that his dark hair wasn't as curly. Detective Gundersen's hair was straight, too, but gray and lay flat on his head like that of the late legendary singer, Mr. Frank Sinatra. My grandmother, who is an actress and knows these things, says Mr. Sinatra's hair was not totally his own. Maybe Detective Gundersen's isn't either, but I'd like to think that the Los Angeles Police Department would insist that their officers eschew such nonessential cosmetic touches.

The horn was a code Detective Gundersen had set up with Mr. B.A. Dawg, who was driving a peach-colored Rolls Royce maybe two car-lengths ahead of us on Sunset. It informed him that the transmission was working well and he could stop testing it with his dreadful singsong.

But he didn't stop.

"*Show some sense,*
"*Keep Mr. Pig on the de-fense.*
"*He comes aroun', puts you down,*
"*Expects to find you shiverin' and shakin'.*
"*Take the pledge, use an edge,*
  cut that mutha oinker up into bacon."

"What the heck's he saying, Mumms?" Gundersen asked.

"You don't wanna know, Herm," Officer Mumms called to him. She smiled at me. "How old are you?"

"Fifteen-and-a-half," I replied truthfully.

"And you don't like rap?"

"Vachel Lindsay is about as far as I go," I said.

"Never heard of her," Officer Mumms said. "But I dig the Dawg man. I hope we can catch the guy messing with him."

Mr. Dawg moved on to another of his ditties, one exploring his total lack of respect for womankind. "He's giving a concert at the Shrine tomorrow night," Officer Mumms said.

"I know," I said.

She leaned toward me and, in a voice loud enough for Mr. Bloodworth to hear, asked, "Your boss like rap?"

Mr. Bloodworth wasn't my boss, exactly. Though officially categorized as a "high school student," I am sort of his apprentice, spending my afternoons, and some school holidays at his detective agency, mainly observing the art of criminology. I also do a little filing and billing, which I was in the middle of, alone in the office, when the call came in from Ms. Lulu Diamond, Mr. Dawg's manager, the day before. If Mr. Bloodworth had been there, he probably would have turned down the job. But he wasn't and so he and I were in the van, sharing an adventure with the members of the Star Squad.

"Does Mr. B. like rap? No," I told Officer Mumms, "rap really isn't his thing. His idea of popular music is 'Moon River.' "

He glared at me with those odd yellow-brown hawk's eyes. "Careful, sis," he said. "You're talking about the late, great Johnny Mercer."

> "*Cops, they got the wrong approach,*
> "*Like the cockroach,*
> "*Crawl around in the dirt,*
> "*Gonna meet up with a hero,*
> > *burn 'em up like Nero,*
> > *and make 'em face the big hurt.*"

"Jeeze," Detective Gundersen said. "If he don't change the tune, I may wind up killing him, myself."

Mr. Bloodworth sighed.

51

★ ★ ★ ★ ★

As I said, the big, rawboned sleuth hadn't wanted to get involved with Mr. Dawg at all. But I'd explained to him that because of his recent illness—he'd been felled by a strain of the Outback flu—the month had been a gloomy one, financially speaking. And there was no sign on the horizon of any other ship coming in.

On arriving at Mr. Dawg's suite at the Beverly-Rodeo Hotel, I must admit to a certain trepidation on my part, too. The place was filled with an assortment of unpleasant people—loud and arrogant men in expensive baggy gym clothes and silver jewelry, caught up in some football epic on TV and totally ignoring their lady friends who, I am sorry to report, were no less anti-social. Nor better dressed.

"Rock and roll trash," Mr. B. muttered to me, and though he was several generations off, his point was well made.

A little pink-cheeked, bespectacled matron in her fifties, her round body covered by a loud Hawaiian muumuu, navigated the crowd gracefully to greet us. "I'm Lulu Diamond," she told us, using a chubby finger to point to the glittering stones embedded in her eyeglass frames.

We exchanged introductions and she asked, "What can I getcha, kid? These bums B.A. calls his friends have cleaned out the portable bar, but I can order up room service."

"I'm fine," I told her.

"You, honey?" she asked Mr. B.

"I'm okay, too," he said scanning the scene. "I don't see your client."

"He's, uh," she pointed to me and winked, "spending quality time with the missus in the bedroom."

The big detective winced. "Yeah, well, Ms. Diamond—"

"Make it Lulu, big guy."

"Lulu, you think you could pry him loose? We ought to get

moving on this, assuming that we're dealing with a real situation."

Lulu frowned and suddenly didn't look so matronly. "B.A. Dawg, with three platinum CDs and the new one going gold after just two weeks, does not have to resort to fake death threats to make headlines."

"I hope not," Mr. Bloodworth said. "Because then we'd be wasting our time."

"I'll go get him," she said.

"There seems to be a lot of violence in the record business," I said, mainly to distract him from the ball game on TV.

"Yeah," he said absently, eyes glazing at the sight of pigskin. "Gangs. Drugs. Good old-fashioned business rivalry. I don't think we're dealing with that here. In fact, I don't know what we're dealing with here."

According to Lulu, Mr. Dawg had received one of those scary notes made up of pasted letters announcing that an organization called The Rap Tribunal had found him guilty of plagiarism. In his ultimate wisdom, he assumed the sender to be a crank, though he should have realized that anyone who went to all the trouble of clipping and pasting that sort of note surely would not go quietly away.

He'd no sooner disposed of the note when the Tribunal gentleman was on the phone, his voice electronically altered, offering Mr. Dawg a choice. He could donate a portion of the profits from his most popular CD, "Smack Attack," to the poor street people from whom he stole most of his lyrics. Or he could die. The amount requested was $250,000 in $100 bills, to be placed in one of those aluminum suitcases.

He had twenty-four hours to get the money and stand by for further instructions. But if he went to the police, he might as well put a gun to his own head.

That's when Lulu dialed the Bloodworth Agency.

Mr. Bloodworth was falling under the spell of the ball game when I spied Lulu waving to us from an open doorway. "We're being summoned," I said.

Mr. Dawg was sitting on a rumpled bed, a man of thirty or so. He was wearing leather pants the color of brown mustard. No shoes. No shirt. He was long and thin and very black. His hair was dyed a bright yellow. And there were enough pieces of metal embedded in his ears and nose to keep him off of planes for the rest of his life.

"You the fake fuzz?" he asked Mr. Bloodworth.

The sleuth allowed he was.

"Blood-worth. I like that. This your lady friend?" Mr. Dawg asked, looking at me.

"Thirty-five years too late for that," Mr. B. said.

"She don't look so young," Mr. Dawg said. "Nasty's only twenty. And she been Mrs. Dawg for two years."

His reference was to the woman seated at the dresser combing her hair. She was nearly as tall as he, and as thin. But there was a languid quality to her, as if she weren't fully awake. I imagine it must have had quite an effect on simple-minded men. She said, "I keep telling you, my name's Nastasia. And it seems like I been with you an eternity, bro."

Mr. Dawg shrugged. "So, you gonna keep me in one piece, Bloodworth?"

"I'll be honest with you, B.A. No one person can guarantee to do that."

"See," Nastasia said. "Told you, Dawgman. Get those cops from last year."

Mr. Bloodworth raised his eyebrows. "What cops would that be?"

"During the tour last year," Lulu said, "we had another

little problem when we hit L.A. One of the former members of the Dawg Posse, that's B.A.'s backup, went a little whacko and made some threats. So we called the cops and they sent us these detectives who specialize in dealing with celebrities."

"The Star Squad," Mr. B. said.

"Yeah. That's them," Nastasia said. "Headed up by this old guy and some young dude."

"Young dude was a little too fresh, you ask me," B.A. said.

"You just a crazy man," Nastasia said. "We oughta get those guys back. They didn't take more than a day to pick Walter up and toss his butt into jail."

"It's the way to go," Mr. Bloodworth said. "If you want me to duplicate the level of protection the cops can give you, I'll have to put on a bunch of other operatives. Could cost you as much as four grand a day."

"That's no good," B.A. Dawg said. "But the man on the phone say no cops."

"They always say that. Cops know how to handle it."

Mr. Dawg snapped his fingers at Lulu and the two of them walked out onto the balcony to discuss the situation.

Nastasia looked me up and down. "What are you playin' at, girl?"

"Beg pardon?"

"What are you doing here?"

"I work with Mr. Bloodworth," I said.

"Yeah? Well, Mr. Blood, here, fits the private eye image, but you, I'd take you for some kinda Spice Girl wannabe."

"Then you'd be making a mistake," I said.

Mr. Dawg and his manager re-entered the room. He snapped his fingers at Mr. Bloodworth. "Cops are in. But I want you to handle it."

"How's that?" Mr. B. asked.

"The cops. I don't like 'em. So I'm payin' you to deal with

'em. Work everything out with them and then tell me."

"Mr. Dawg," I asked, "could it be your former employee, Walter, trying to get your attention again?"

He shrugged. "Walter's crazy enough to do it, I guess."

"Maybe the cops still have a line on him," Mr. Bloodworth said.

"C'mon, tall, blond and rugged," Lulu said to Mr. Bloodworth. "Let's go talk money."

Later, when he and I were driving downtown to Parker Center where the Star Squad offices are located, Mr. Bloodworth said, "Herm Gundersen and I go back a ways. This should be a snap; we'll just let him do all the work."

In point of fact, he and Detective Gundersen had gone through the police academy together. So there was none of the antagonism a private detective sometimes encounters when dealing with lawmen.

"The Dawgman again, huh?" Detective Gundersen said. "Hear that, Lucas?"

Detective Lucas looked up from his desk four feet away. "Who's he pissed off this time?"

"Maybe the same guy you arrested last year," Mr. B. suggested.

The handsome young detective picked up the phone and quickly ascertained that Walter Lipton, the recalcitrant ex-employee, had been released from prison only three weeks before.

"Talk about your likely suspects," Detective Gundersen said. "Well, we'll take over from here, Leo."

"That'd be fine with me, Herm, but Dawg said he'd like us to stick around."

Detective Gundersen hesitated, then smiled, "Sure, buddy. You and the kid are welcome to observe a crack team in action. Lucas, slap on that charming smile of yours and let's show 'em how we handle international celebrities in this man's town."

So we'd "observed" them shooing away the freeloaders at the hotel, setting up the phone taps, arranging for counterfeit bills to be placed in an aluminum suitcase along with a tracking device, and being generally obsequious in the presence of Mr. Dawg, his skinny sullen wife and Lulu.

To give the Star Squad their due when the representative of the Rap Tribunal finally called, they certainly leapt into action. Unfortunately, the call had been made on a cellular phone and was therefore untraceable. But at least we had a tape of the conversation and didn't have to rely on Mr. Dawg's rather short attention span.

The gentleman from the Rap Tribunal informed Mr. Dawg that he had thirty minutes to get into his Rolls Royce with the suitcase and drive to a public telephone at an address on Sunset Boulevard. Further instructions would be forthcoming.

So there we were, tagging along, being regaled by the so-called rapmaster's poetic but addled view of life. Suddenly, he stopped mid-rhyme to declare, "Mus' be the place."

He pulled to the curb at a bus stop in front of a sidewalk shop called Café Coffee and got out of the Rolls. The pay phone was just at the edge of the café's patio which was filled with folks satisfying their caffeine fix alfresco.

There were no other spaces, legal or illegal, for the van, so Detective Lucas drove about a quarter of a block past the Rolls and, double-parked. Up ahead was an unmarked sedan, stopped in a similar position. Its occupants were four other members of the Star Squad. They were a bit too far away to keep Mr. Dawg in view, but we could see him, resplendent in his powder blue leather jumpsuit, standing at the phone.

"Would you look at the hot babes at that coffee place?" Detective Lucas said. "Damn, I love L.A."

"Keep your roving eye on the Dawgman, huh?" his boss asked.

Thanks to the transmitter taped to his chest, we could hear sidewalk noises, the whistle of the wind and, eventually, a ringing phone. "Yeah, it's me," we heard him say. We could not hear the caller at all.

"Hold on," Mr. Dawg said. He reached under the ledge of the booth and removed a small object that had been taped there. "Got it." It was a cellular phone.

Detective Lucas said, "Check out the babe and the guy sitting at the second table over from B.A."

A young African-American couple seemed very interested in Mr. Dawg. In any other city in the free world, it would not seem unusual for people to be gawking at a blonde African-American recording star wearing powder blue leather, tearing something from beneath a pay telephone ledge. But this was Hollywood. And none of the other patrons of Café Coffee was giving him a second's notice.

As he hopped back into his Rolls, the couple stood up from their table. The man tossed a few bills down and they both ran for their car.

"What now, Herm?" Detective Lucas asked.

"Wait and watch, lover boy."

Mr. Dawg pulled out into traffic. From our speakers, his voice blared, "Man say he'll call me on the phone, tell me where to go."

The couple got into a little red BMW. When they passed us, heading after Mr. Dawg, Detective Gundersen yelled, "Let's roll."

"I take it neither of those people is the guy who gave Dawg trouble last year," Mr. Bloodworth said.

"Lipton? Naw," Detective Gundersen said. "He's probably manning the phone."

"That's a heck of a bright red car they're using to collect loot," Mr. Bloodworth observed.

"Amateurs," Detective Gundersen sneered. "Mumms, run a check on that license, if you please."

It was blissfully quiet in the Rolls. Mr. Dawg evidently was too caught up in the moment to be thinking about rapping. But Detective Lucas took up the musical slack, humming nervously, oblivious to the scowls being sent his way by his boss.

Mr. Bloodworth picked up on the detective's melody. We listened to their duet for a few minutes, until Detective Gundersen growled, "Could we can the concert?"

Mr. Bloodworth looked at me and shook his head sadly. "You don't like that, you don't like good music," he muttered.

"Another of your Johnny Mercer songs?" I asked.

"Close. Bobby Troup. Route 66."

He started to recite the lyrics, which sounded to my ears almost like rap, except they were much more whimsical (rhyming "Arizona" with "Winona," for example). The ringing of Mr. Dawg's cellular interrupted him.

We heard the rapper say, "Okay. Make the next turn and head back to the ocean."

The unmarked sedan in the lead must've gotten the message because we saw it head into the left lane just in front of the Rolls. The red Beamer was directly behind Mr. Dawg. We were several cars behind it. "How you doin' on that license check, Mumms?"

"We'll get it when we get it, Herm," she said.

Our little caravan made the turn and continued west on Sunset for about a mile when the cellular rang again. "Okay,"

Mr. Dawg said, "I turn down Doheny to Santa Monica Boulevard and keep going to the ocean." He was silent for a beat, then added, "Sure, I got the cash. I'm co-operatin'. No, sir, no cops nohow."

Officer Mumms emitted a little chuckle. "Isn't he somethin'?" she asked.

We moved along Santa Monica Boulevard, past the Century City shopping center and on under the San Diego Freeway. Past old movie houses, rows and rows of small businesses, restaurants.

The temperature dropped several degrees when we moved through the seacoast town of Santa Monica. I was starting to smell ocean salt in the air when the phone rang again.

"Right," Mr. Dawg said. "I turn right on Ocean, take the incline to the Coast Highway and keep goin' 'til I see the sign for Topanga Canyon. Then head up the Canyon. Why we going to all this trouble? Lemme jus' give you the damn money. I got me a concert tonight. I . . . Damn, he hung up on me."

Detective Gundersen scowled. "It would've been simpler to have us just stay on Sunset. Why the circle route?"

"Must be making sure the rap man is all by his lonesome," Detective Lucas said.

"Mumms, tell Maclin to press the pedal and go on up Topanga and wait." Detective Maclin was in the lead car. "Lucas, you'd better pull back as far as you can. We don't want to spook those folks in the red car. And, Mumms, can't we find out who the hell they are?"

"Searches take time," Officer Mumms said.

The couple in the red car didn't seem to care if we spooked them or not. They remained on Mr. Dawg's tail up into the Canyon.

My grandmother loves to tell horror stories about gruesome crimes that have taken place in Topanga back in the 1960s way before I was born, during that odd historic time of social unrest. As we drove through, it didn't look dangerous at all. Just another moderately populated rustic canyon.

Mr. Dawg's phone rang again. This time the instruction was to turn off into Calico Canyon.

Unfortunately, the instruction came too late for the lead car. The Rolls made the turn, followed by the red Beamer. Then, after a considerable distance, us. Detective Maclin and his men were now last in line as we climbed along a small road through the relatively uninhabited, tree shaded canyon.

Higher and higher we went along the twisting macadam, barely keeping the little red car in sight and not seeing the Rolls at all.

The cellular rang and Mr. Dawg said, rather waspishly, "Okay. I'm stoppin'. And I'm tossin' the suitcase . . . Now what? . . . You sure I can get out of here goin' up? . . . Okay, you the man."

We rounded a curve and saw the Rolls pulling away.

But the red Beamer had stopped. The male, who'd been driving, got out and was at the side of the road, bending down to pick up the suitcase.

"It's a go-go-go," Detective Gundersen yelled.

"Book 'em, Dano," Officer Mumms said to Detective Maclin.

The officer, Mr. Bloodworth and I remained in the car. We watched as the plainclothes policemen ran to the man holding the suitcase. The woman threw open her car door and got out, rushing to her companion.

"LAPD," Detective Gundersen growled, "Drop the money, boy."

"Boy?" the young man shouted back. "Who the hell . . . ?"

Then he made a big mistake. He threw the suitcase at the detective.

Suddenly several other people were on him, pummeling him with their fists.

"Jee-zus," Officer Mumms said.

"This is bad news," Mr. Bloodworth said, getting out of the van. "Stay here, Sara."

As he ran toward the melee, Officer Mumms' radio began to squawk and a static-y voice informed us that, according to its plates, the red BMW was licensed to a Mr. and Mrs. Joseph Laurence of Mill Valley.

"Where you goin', girl?" Officer Mumms asked me. "Your boss said stay."

"I took no vow of obedience to him," I told her.

Mr. Bloodworth had pulled one of the detectives off of the young man. And was getting a fist to the side of his head for his trouble.

Screaming at them, the young woman kicked another detective in the shin and received an elbow in the chest that sent her to the ground.

I ran to their car, looked in. Then I quickly opened the driver's door and kept pressing the horn until I had everybody's attention.

"They're tourists," I shouted.

"Huh?" Detective Gundersen said.

"Tourists. From Mill Valley. They've got luggage in the back of their car and highway maps in the front. Look," I held up a pair of Mickey Mouse ears. "They've been to Disneyland."

Officer Mumms had left the van, too. She moved to Mrs. Laurence and was helping her from the ground.

The young man pulled away from Detective Lucas' grip, wiped his bloody nose on his shirt and staggered to his wife.

"You all right, baby?"

"Jus' got the wind knocked out of her," Officer Mumms said.

Mrs. Laurence nodded in agreement.

"You bastards are crazy," Joseph Laurence of Mill Valley said to all of them. "I'm gonna sue your ass off."

"Yeah?" Detective Gundersen said. "First you're gonna have to explain to us crazy bastards what the hell you tourists are doing out here with that metal suitcase?"

The young man lost just an inch of attitude. "My wife and I are having a cup of coffee wondering how to spend our last afternoon in L.A. when there's B.A. Dawg, himself, right there on the street. The rappin' rap master. So I figure, let's check out what the Dawgman's up to."

"That brings us to the suitcase."

"We're behind the man, see him toss something from his Rolls. I tell my wife, hell, B.A. Dawg may not want whatever that is, but for the rest of us, it's a solid gold souvenir."

Detective Gundersen looked dubious, but he said, "We'll check out your story."

"Check out my story? You sure as hell will. Right after I sue you and everybody else for beating on me and my wife."

The detective shifted his gaze from the battered Laurences and scanned the area. I wondered if he might be checking for a video camera. In a flat voice, he said, "We're pretty sensitive to stalking out here, pal. Got all kind of laws against it. So I'm giving you two choices—you can let us fix up your scrapes and bruises while we're checking out your story. Or you can keep mouthin' off about lawsuits and we'll throw you and the little lady into the tank for stalking and harassing Mr. Dawg."

I hit the horn again.

Everyone looked my way. Detective Gundersen seemed particularly peeved. "What now?" he shouted.

"Speaking of Mr. Dawg, aren't we forgetting something?"

In an absolutely horrific piece of bad timing, from the distance came the unmistakable sound of a gunshot.

Shouting orders for the others to stay with the Laurences, Detective Gundersen ran back to the van, followed by Detective Lucas. And me and Mr. Bloodworth.

Detective Lucas eased around the red BMW, slightly scraping the side of the van on the canyon wall before zooming up the road.

Half a mile or so later, we came upon the Rolls sitting still, its engine purring. I started to open the van door, but Mr. Bloodworth grabbed my arm. The two policemen had their pistols drawn and were searching the area through the van's windows.

Eventually, Detective Gundersen said, "The rest of you stay here."

He slipped from the van and, head moving from side to side like a radarscope, he approached the Rolls. He stopped, turned and stared up the canyon wall, then put his pistol back into its holster. He opened the Rolls' passenger door and bent into the vehicle. A few seconds later, the pale exhaust clouds ceased. Detective Gundersen backed out of the car and, looking at Detective Lucas, made a gun with his thumb and forefinger and pantomimed shooting himself in the temple.

Mr. Bloodworth felt it was his duty to notify the widow Dawg.

But by the time we got to the suite at the Beverly-Rodeo Hotel, the news had already broken. The widow was in black—a lacy, sort of see-through outfit, but definitely black—holding a hankie to her red-rimmed eyes.

She thanked Mr. Bloodworth for doing his best to save her

husband's life. Lulu Diamond wasn't quite as forgiving. "I hope you don't expect to get paid for letting poor B.A. take one in the head," she said. "You're lucky I don't sue. Maybe I will."

"You do what you want," he told her. He was feeling very low about the way things turned out.

As we started for the door, Mrs. Dawg called out, "Hey, Mr. Blood, don't listen to her. I'm grateful you did what you could for my husband. You'll get your money. It wasn't your fault the police panicked Walter into shooting B.A."

"It was his fault the bungling cops came into it," Lulu grumbled.

"No. That was my suggestion, Lulu," Mrs. Dawg said. "My fault."

"But when somebody doesn't deliver—"

"Pay the man, Lulu."

"Look, it's my opinion—"

"But it's my money."

Grumbling, Lulu Diamond went to the desk, opened a checkbook and began scribbling on it.

The phone rang and Mrs. Dawg said, "Could you get that, Mr. Blood? I'm not up to phone talk."

Mr. Bloodworth, looking even more uncomfortable than usual, lifted the receiver. "This is, ah, the Dawg suite . . . oh, hi, Herm."

The big detective listened a bit, then his face registered surprise. "Damn. That was fast . . . No kidding. Yeah, I'll tell her. Thanks."

He placed the phone back on its cradle and turned to Mrs. Dawg. "That was the cops, ma'am," he said. "They found the guy who murdered your husband. Walter Lipton."

"Oh?" She said it as though it didn't matter much.

"He put up a fight and they had to shoot him."

"Is he dead?" she asked.

"Uh huh."

"Too damn bad, huh?" she said and went into the bed-room, closing the door behind her.

Lulu ripped the check from her book, waved it in the air and handed it to Mr. Bloodworth. "You oughta be ashamed to take this."

"Right," Mr. B. said, jerking the paper from her fingers and slipping it into his wallet.

"So they caught and killed the schlemiel who put an end to my meal ticket," Lulu said. "Big friggin' deal."

"Whew," Mr. Bloodworth said, when we were back in his car. "Tough racket."

As we drove toward the apartment I share with Grams, I opened his glove compartment and began digging through his music tapes. Finally, I found one titled "Kicks on 66, the songs of Bobby Troup."

I slipped it into his cassette player and heard a man with a very pleasant voice sing the title number. "You're right," I told Mr. B, "it's a neat song."

"Troup's a real talent. Used to be married to Julie London."

The name meant nothing to me. "According to the song, Route 66 runs from Chicago to L.A.," I said. "Where is it out here, exactly?"

The big detective scratched his head. "Darned if I know. I think they renamed it or something."

"I'll have to look it up," I said.

"The only thing I have to do is deposit this check," he said. "And hope it clears."

I imagine he must have spent some of it in his dim bars because he seemed a little slurry when he arrived at his apartment at ten that night. I'd been phoning him since four in the afternoon.

"Wha's so 'portant?" he wanted to know.

When I told him, he was silent for a few seconds. Then he said, "Could be a coinc'ence."

"A coincidence? Not likely."

"Hmmm. How can we be sure?"

I gave him a suggestion. I'd been thinking the problem through for five hours.

By the time the detectives, Gundersen and Lucas, arrived at the Beverly-Rodeo Hotel at shortly before eleven, Mr. Bloodworth seemed to have sobered up a bit. The lawmen were totally sober. And angry. "Leo, what the hell is this all about? We found the rifle that killed Dawg in Lipton's apartment. He's been IDed as the purchaser of the cell phone. All that was hanging fire was a checkup on the Laurences. That came in and we are now confident that Lipton was acting alone."

"He's dead," Detective Lucas added. "The case is closed."

"But Mr. Lipton wasn't acting alone," I said. "Someone was working with him, someone who could provide him with Mr. Dawg's suite telephone number, someone who knew that Mr. Dawg was familiar enough with Southern California streets and byways to follow rather cryptic directions."

Detective Gundersen shook his head and turned to Mr. Bloodworth. "Leo, I hope we're not here just because of this kid's fantasies."

"Serendipity's pretty good at this sort of thing," Mr. Bloodworth said. "Let's go on up to the suite. The ladies are waiting for us."

"You bothered that poor woman?" Detective Lucas said.

"Interrupted her mourning?"

"She'll rest better when we clean this up," Mr. Bloodworth said, entering the hotel.

On the way up in the elevator, Detective Lucas asked me, "So, who do you think was helping Lipton?"

"Lulu Diamond, of course," I said.

The young policeman raised an eyebrow. "Why 'of course'?"

"She had a strong motive," Mr. Bloodworth said. "I checked in with this guy in New York who's on top of the music business. Says Dawg had feelers out for a new manager. Not only was Lulu going to lose her main client, the insurance policy she's been carrying on his life would be canceled."

"How big's the policy, Leo?"

"Two mil," Mr. Bloodworth said.

Detective Gundersen let out a low whistle. Detective Lucas looked amazed.

The two women were waiting for us. Not cheerily. Nastasia Dawg sat on the sofa, a wine colored robe wrapped over what appeared to be a satin nightgown. Lulu was dressed in yet another muumuu, this one with large blood-red flowers against a yellow background.

"Let's get this over with," she said waspishly, "I need my beauty sleep."

"Okay, Lulu," Mr. Bloodworth said, as planned, "these officers are here to arrest you in connection with the murder of B.A. Dawg."

Lulu's mouth dropped. And Nastasia Dawg seemed to shake off her languor for the first time, her eyes saucer-wide.

"You son of a buck," Lulu shouted at Detective Lucas. "You sold me out."

The handsome detective couldn't have been more surprised if Lulu's skin had peeled away exposing a Martian underneath. "Are you nuts?" he wailed.

"Yeah," Lulu said, advancing on him. "Nuts for thinking I could count on you."

"Hold on," Detective Gundersen shouted. "Mrs. Diamond, you're saying Lucas is involved in Dawg's murder?"

"Involved? He planned it."

"She's demented," Detective Lucas whined. "I don't even know her."

"You say that now, you bum," Lulu snarled. "But on the phone it was 'Lulu, honey, it's a perfect plan. I got this nut case Lipton all primed to pull the trigger. He's spent the last year getting crazier and crazier. All we've gotta do is get the rapmeister within fifty yards of him.' "

"This is insane," Detective Lucas protested.

"You located Lipton pretty quick today, Lucas," Detective Gundersen said. "And it was you shot him dead."

The young detective looked from his boss to Lulu to Nastasia.

"Stand up guy, huh?" Lulu said with contempt. She turned to us. "That's how he described himself last year when you cops took care of Walter Lipton the first time."

"You two have been planning this for a year?" Mr. Bloodworth asked.

"His plan," she said. "But I went along. I guess we can forget all about that insurance money now, huh, lover?"

Detective Lucas' hand went for his gun, but Mr. Bloodworth was too fast for him. One punch and the younger man was on the floor and Mr. B. was holding the weapon.

Detective Gundersen looked down at his partner and said, "You have the right to remain silent . . ."

As he worked his way through the Miranda litany, his

young detective looked past him, staring at Nastasia Dawg. "Tell 'em," Detective Lucas shouted over the recitation of his rights. "Tell 'em, damnit."

"I don't know what you're talking about, mister," the sultry woman replied.

"I'm talking about us."

"You and Lulu?" Nastasia looked genuinely confused. But Mr. Bloodworth and I knew that to be a pose.

"Me and you," the no longer very handsome policeman screamed.

"Man's pathetic," Nastasia said, turning to leave the room.

"Yeah, I guess I am," Detective Lucas said bitterly. "I was dumb enough to fall for that 'my husband beats me' routine. We had to kill him before he killed her. That's what she got me to believe. Then we'd be in velvet. All that loot. We'd live happily ever after. Just another goddamned pipe dream."

He grabbed Detective Gundersen's arm. "You know I'm not lying to you, Herm," he pleaded. "I wouldn't have done what I did for some ugly fat broad."

Lulu Diamond's eyes narrowed.

"I guess I do know that much about you, Lucas," the older detective said sadly. "Leo, you want to keep him and Mrs. Dawg covered while I phone for somebody to come take 'em away?"

Nastasia sneered at Detective Lucas. "It was a setup. Lulu's working with them, you vain jackass. Why is it I always wind up with fools?"

"Lulu, you were terrific," I said. "You should have been an actress."

"I tried that," she said. "But I never was much good. Guess I was waiting for that perfect role. Thanks for giving it to me, Bloodworth."

"Don't thank me," he said. "It was Sara who wrote the script."

Nastasia turned to me. "Of course, it was you. And tell me, little Spice Girl, was it something I said?"

"No. Well, Mr. Dawg did indicate he was jealous of you and Detective Lucas. But, actually, it had more to do with our driving around today. Detective Lucas did something that indicated he knew where we were headed even before Mr. Lipton conveyed that information to Mr. Dawg."

"That's a lie," Detective Lucas said.

"You wish," I told him. "When we were traveling on Sunset Boulevard, you knew we would eventually drive out of our way to take Santa Monica Boulevard to the ocean."

"I knew that?" Detective Lucas said. "You need help, kid."

"One of us does. According to the Route 66 page on the Internet, the highway runs along Santa Monica Boulevard and ends at the ocean."

"Yeah. I know that. I once drove 66 all the way from Santa Monica to Albuquerque. So what?"

"So while we were still on Sunset, headed away from the ocean, you started humming Mr. Bobby Troup's famous song. You had Route 66 on your mind at a time when only those who planned Mr. Dawg's murder knew that's where we were headed."

"Another fool, just like B.A.," Nastasia said.

"But with better taste in music," I said. "Unfortunately for you both."

71

Sad-Eyed Blonde

Los Angeles, 1940.

The thing about having an office on Hollywood Boulevard is that you never know what's going to come calling. Even if you're six flights up. That humid Monday morning, the list began with a butterfly. It cleared the sill, maneuvered past the lifeless curtain and paused to check out the room before committing itself further. It took in walls the color of a jaundice victim, a desk that had more scars than Primo Carnera's nose, a rump-sprung client's chair, five pond-green filing cabinets, three of them as empty as my stomach, and me, leaning back in a swivel chair that squeaked like a mouse that had expected Swiss cheese and got farina.

In spite of everything, the butterfly decided to stick around. It soared to the ceiling, skimmed the cobwebs, then did a rollover and dived for the floor where it nestled on the edge of the worn red carpet. It had just settled in when a pair of black and white spectators waltzed through the door and sent it off to bug Valhalla.

The two-tone Sunday dogs were only a part of my visitor's sartorial splendor. Accompanying them were a wide-brim Panama with a pink band, a nutmeg brown silk suit, a dark red shirt, and a white dickey-sized tie with pink bubbles on it that matched the hatband. The guy's vaguely cherubic face was pink, too, and freshly barbered. His sunburned nose, which should have been on a larger, fatter man, was as red as a beefsteak tomato.

73

His nervous eyes shifted from me to the squashed butterfly. He said, "Aw, Christ," and dropped to one knee. He used a polished fingernail to scrape what was left of the bug from the carpet, whipped out a pink display hanky and rested the remains on it. "Aw, Christ," he repeated.

I watched him with a certain sense of wonder as he brought the handkerchief litter to my desk and placed it carefully on the glass top before sinking with a sigh onto the client chair.

"He was a beauty, too," he said. "It's not like we got so much beauty in the world, we can afford to waste a little. I'm a goddamn Jonah is what I am."

I removed my dead pipe from the ashtray, picked up his handkerchief and dropped the ex-butterfly among the ashes and butts. I dumped the whole mess into the wastebasket and handed him back his pink linen. "Stir seems to have bared your poetic soul, Johnny. Or is this a new grift?"

He gave me a smile as thin as boardinghouse milk and said, "So sue me if I like insects. Try five years doubled up in a ten-foot cage with an ex-pin jabber who can't do nothing but play nose checkers, and see if you don't start giving pet names to cockroaches."

"I'll take your word for it," I said, waiting for him to get around to the reason he'd dropped by.

As he patted his handkerchief back into his coat pocket, he scanned the room. "You ain't exactly conquering the world, are you, pally?"

"I'll leave that to Mr. Hitler and see how far he gets with it. Are we just waltzing here, or is something special going to happen when the band stops playing?"

His smile grew wider under his bright red nose. "Kay'll be up in a sec. She stopped off at the Madison to grab some smokes, say hello to the old gang. She tole me how you helped out while I was inside."

Kay was Johnny Horne's wife, a tall blonde with sad, China-blue eyes, who used to be a good cop. Her problem was, she had lousy taste in men. Johnny wasn't the worst of them. But he was determined to bounce checks for a living even though he had no aptitude for it. So Kay had been forced to turn in her tin and get a job selling smokes at the Madison House while Johnny spent most of their wedded years in San Quentin sewing mailbags. That's where he'd been when Kay had brought me into a situation involving stolen pearls.

It hadn't been quite the cakewalk she'd described; but four or five stiffs later, we wound up splitting twenty-five grand that the insurance company had posted for the recovery of the teardrops.

Johnny Horne ran his little pinkie along a crater a cigarette had scorched in the desk. "You musta put your share of the loot in the bank, huh, pally? Saving it for a rainy day."

"I keep it in my bathtub in dimes and quarters so I can run my fingers through it on slow nights."

I was about to ask him how Kay was when I found out for myself. "Hi, stranger," she drawled from the doorway. The last I'd seen of her, she'd been slightly seedy and as glum as St. Agnes on a cloudy day, even with a handbag full of twelve thousand five-hundred dollars. In the harsh sunlight that sneaked past the drapes, she looked like a new woman. Her blue eyes were so bright they glittered, and her simple aqua dress fit her lanky frame like pants on a lamb chop. I wondered if the reward money had been responsible for the changeover, or if it was Johnny getting his wings.

He hopped from the chair and held it out for her as carefully as if it were a Chippendale.

Kay asked, "How much have I missed?"

"We haven't left the starting gate," I told her.

Johnny cleared his throat and said: "Waitin' on you, angel cake."

Angel cake leaned back in the chair. "You still hide your gargle in that desk drawer, honey?"

"Right next to the knitting," I said, pulling out the Old Forester and a couple of glasses. Ever the proper host, I poured them each a shot and took mine from the bottle. Johnny sipped his carefully. Kay downed hers with a little chuckle, coughed once, and said, "I figure we owe you this one."

"You don't owe me a thing."

"You split that insurance loot right down the middle; and hell knows, you did all of the work and took all of the knocks."

"History doesn't pay the rent," I said. "So the hell with history."

"This one'll make us all fat as geese," she said earnestly. Johnny's eyes ping-ponged from her to me.

"Maybe I'm trying to lose weight."

Johnny chuckled nervously. He shook his head, and his Panama wiggled like it had caught a breeze. "Pally, the tag on this could be as much as one hundred gees."

I smiled at them both. "As much as that, huh?"

Kay started to straighten the papers on my desk. Either she was a compulsive cleaner, or she was being evasive. "Are you in?" she asked.

"Not yet. But I love a good story." I had nothing pressing. The chicken pot pie wouldn't be ready at Musso's for another two hours.

She pulled a pack of gaspers from her purse, peeled away the cellophane, tore off a neat square of silver paper, and deposited it into my empty ashtray, all in one graceful motion. "A little touch I picked up pushing tobacco down at the Madison," she said, offering me a nail.

I used the desk lighter on her cigarette, then mine, and relit Johnny's. No sense tempting fate. After we'd blown enough smoke in each other's faces, Kay said, "Ever hear of the Jeweled Skull of Lhasa?"

I replied, "You stepped in what?"

"The Jeweled Skull of Lhasa. About the size of an ostrich egg. Belonged to this Holy Joe in Tibet a couple of lifetimes ago. His tribe had inlaid it with sparklers, rubies, the works. A British expedition stumbled on it, twenty or twenty-five years back. One of the Brits pinched it when nobody was looking."

"Gee," I said. "Is there a curse on it? People dropping like flies just from the sight of it?"

Kay said, "Crack wise all you want, honey. But a Warbucks in Frisco wound up with it on his mantelpiece. And, though some may consider it to be in bad taste, he was goddamned fond of it. So when it got lifted he posted one hundred grand for its return."

"And you know where it is?"

"No," she said. "But I know somebody who knows."

"How'd you manage that?"

Her blue eyes sparkled. "The years I spent on the force count for something," she said. "I still got friends downtown."

Johnny Horne bent down and kissed his wife's cheek.

"An L.A. cop knows the whereabouts of a priceless doodad and he talks to you about it?" I wondered.

"That's the beauty part," Johnny said. "He can't move on it."

Johnny's grin was as big as his head was empty. I turned to Kay. "I guess I missed a salient point."

Kay stared at me for a beat. "I . . . the cop's name is Beaudry."

In my head, a nickel started rolling toward a slot.

She continued, "You must remember him from when you were working for the D.A."

The nickel dropped. A scarecrow with sawed-off hair and a chin like a towel rack who was always in Dutch with the D.A., Harold Wilde. Usually had his nose in a book. The day Wilde handed me my walking papers Beaudry looked up from his novel to grumble, " 'And so proceed ad infinitum.' " I didn't know what the hell that was supposed to mean and was not inclined at the time to care very much.

"If Beaudry's got a line on the skull, he's holding all the aces," I said. "Why deal me in?"

She said, "Because I told him we can trust you."

I grinned at her. "Yeah. But other than that."

She smiled back. "Beaudry knows where the thief is holed up. But, being a cop, he can't front the recovery. His boss, Captain Maclin, would get too curious."

"Maclin would also want a piece of the reward, like maybe ninety-nine percent," Johnny added.

"That's why Beaudry came to me. He'd heard about the recovery of those pearls. And how the payoff went down."

I exhaled a little smoke and looked from her to Johnny. She patted her husband's hand and said, "Sweetheart, would you take a little stroll? Then we'll have us a nice lunch somewhere."

Johnny leaned forward and touched her cheek. He cleared his throat and croaked, "I think I'll take a stroll." At the door he added, "Sorry about your butterfly, shamus."

"He wasn't mine, Johnny. He dropped by to visit my blue-bottle flies."

"Whatever." He left us with another of his halfhearted, crooked smiles.

Kay wasted a minute after the outer door clicked shut before she said, "The last stretch took its toll. Johnny came out of Grey Castle like Ferdinand. He'd rather smell the flowers. But even if he wanted in on this, Beaudry would keep him out. You know how cops are about cons. So I suggested that you front the deal, and that was swell with Beaudry. He likes you."

"That must be why he looked the other way when Wilde lowered the boom on me."

"I wouldn't know about that. Anyway, wasn't somebody just telling me how useful history is?"

"Good point. How do we carve up the bird?"

She hesitated, then said, "Beaudry wants half. You and I split the rest."

Twenty-five grand. Enough for a good day's work. I nodded.

Kay relaxed and tried a smile.

"You look good," I told her.

"It comes and it goes."

I poured her another finger of hooch and we toasted the future. Then she turned off the smile and said, "Beaudry's playing this close to the vest. He's kept me in the dark about the who and the where. You'll get it all tonight at his house— a bungalow over in Culver City, by the bakery. He'll be there by eight. I'll phone him you're coming."

I stared at her while she wrote out the address. The situation seemed a little more complicated than necessary, but that was typical of Beaudry. No matter how many times his backside got gnawed on by D.A. Harry Wilde because of it, Beaudry never did things the simple way. He preferred to circle a problem and attack it from some odd angle. By that time, it was usually too late.

I took another swig. Recovering the skull was going to be a snap. Sure it was. I put that thought in my back pocket near my wallet and told Kay that Johnny was making noises like he might be staying on this side of the gate for a while.

She shrugged. "Maybe. But you know what they say about old habits, honey. You can't beat 'em to death with a crowbar."

They were having some sort of do at M. G. M. studios, and Washington Boulevard, which was usually pretty empty at that time of night, was teeming with sleek limousines driven by sleek chauffeurs. Maybe President Roosevelt was in town. Maybe Greta Garbo had finally decided she wanted company.

The snarl made me ten minutes late for Beaudry. His bungalow was a fading matchbox on a patchy street full of potholes and weird ideas. Somebody had painted several trees bright yellow. Another had stuck baby dolls all over the top of his Packard. Maybe it was the air. Three blocks away, the Bialy Brothers Best Bread building, a place the size of an airplane hangar, was filling the still, humid night with bakery smells. It was the heady kind of odor that reminded you what the world was like when you were young. Which can be a pleasant thing. Or it can be murder.

There was a dim light inside Beaudry's, and the sound of tinny laughter. I walked past a parched lawn and a weed garden to a screen porch and dusted the door with my knuckles. Inside the house a familiar voice said, "Rochester, have you pressed my tuxedo pants?"

I called out, "Beaudry?"

"Not yet, Mr. Benny. Fella who rented 'em hasn't brought 'em back yet."

More laughter.

I slipped the .38 Colt Super Match from its shoulder holster and tried the screen door. It opened.

"Well, call him and tell him to bring 'em back now. I'm

due at the Colmans in an hour."

I stepped onto a neat little porch with two white rockers and a metal glider.

"Can't call him, Mr. Benny."

"Well, why not?"

"I'm all out of nickels."

I moved through the open front door into a large living room illuminated only by the orange dial of a Philco console. The radio laughter subsided just as the shiny waxed floor creaked under my feet and I heard the click of a hammer being cocked.

"Beaudry?" I asked hopefully, not moving.

"That you, shamus?" came the baritone reply. "I must've drifted off. Lemme get rid of the noise."

A light went on in the corner of the room and Beaudry's scarecrow figure shuffled past me. His bare feet and ankles showed under pants that were too short for him. A white shirt hung down over his belt and flapped around his butt. His gun was still in his hand. I didn't put mine away either.

He clicked off the radio, stuck the gun in his belt, and yawned. I took a quick look around as I holstered my .38. The place could have stood in for a Christian Science Reading Room. One wall was filled with books. Newspapers and magazines were piled neatly on a shiny oak table next to the radio. On the coffee table by the couch an open volume rested. George Santayana's "The Realm of the Spirit," whatever that was.

I asked him if he read much.

He paused to look at his library and shrugged. "Like the feller said, 'Reading maketh a full man.' Sides, as you well know, most police work'd bore the horns off a Billy goat. So I read. Been doing it since my wife passed away. Eleven years, now. C'mon. I'll get us some milk and cookies."

81

I followed him through a neat little dining room with a polished hardwood table and six matching chairs. A bouquet of buttercups and baby's breath sat in a glass vase on a matching sideboard. Past that was the kitchen. White walls. Black and white checkerboard tile floor. A set of dirty dishes rested on a porcelain sink.

He found a bottle of Old Canterbury in the cupboard and dragged it and two tumblers over to a small wooden breakfast table where a book rested beside another vase, this one full of bright red wildflowers, the kind they call desert paintbrush.

Beaudry poured two heavy shots and said, "To crime, huh, shamus?"

I clicked my tumbler against his and wet the back of my throat with the harsh alcohol.

He emptied his glass, made a face, then let out his breath. "It's all in there," he said, indicating the book.

It wasn't a new edition. The blue jacket was battered and worn. The drawing on it was of a black bird and a hand emerging from water holding coins and jewelry.

"This is supposed to tell me how to find a holy man's skull?" I asked.

"Have you read it?"

Actually, I had. I'd heard that its author, Dashiell Hammett, was an ex-Pinkerton, and that had made me curious enough to plunk down the two dollars. I'd liked it, a hell of a lot more than I'd liked the film they made of it with a Latin-lover type as the sleuth, Sam Spade. I heard the Hollywood boys gave it another try a year ago. That time they changed Spade's name. One day they'll learn that some books will never make a good movie.

"I don't see what this's got to do with the price of heads," I told Beaudry.

He grinned and filled our glasses. "There's a lot in there Hammett didn't make up, exactly."

I cocked an eye. "You mean the dame? Brigid whatever?"

"Well, he made her up from two dames he knew. And the fat man was somebody he followed for Pinkerton. It's the black bird I'm talking about. The falcon. It was supposed to have been a gift from the Order of the Hospital of St. John of Jerusalem to Emperor Charles V. A gold falcon encrusted with jewels as a sort of rent payment for their occupation of the island of Malta."

Just listening to him made my throat dry, so I took another pull at the hooch and said, "I think you been reading a little too much, pal."

"Maybe," he said. "But I never heard of a guy going broke because he read too much. You don't want to hear any more, adios, brother."

When I didn't ankle, he continued. "There never were any gold falcons. Historians like Jonathan Theil have written that the birds the Hospitalers gave in those days were made of feathers and claws, not precious metals. What got Hammett thinking about jewels was an ancient skull filled with diamonds and rubies. He saw it in San Francisco in the twenties, in the possession of a heavy holder named Grunwald who'd bought it off of a limey named Forbes-Ralston whose father had looted it from Tibet.

"Grunwald, who owns about five square blocks along Market Street, got his mansion broken into seven years ago. The skull was among the loot. The Frisco cops caught one of the crib crackers when he tried to fence some of the glitter. A little gyp known as the Midget Bandit. He'd been in and out of Q. since twenty-three, when he got nabbed with his mitt in the till of a gas station in Stockton."

"Are we getting to the point, Beaudry? Because if not,

we're going to need another bottle."

"The point is, the Midget is still in Q., and he never spilled on his partner. But I know the bustard's name and I know where he's hanging his turban these days."

"Mind telling me how you came by all this information?"

He grinned at me. "A night three years ago, my partner, Ray Doyle, and I were sent out to Freddie March's house to check a disturbance. There was a hell of a party going on. Flynn was there, and a bunch of writers. This Fitzgerald guy. And Ernest Hemingway. And Hammett, drunk as the well-known skunk, and shouting that Hemingway didn't know nothing about women or how to write about women. Hemingway was responding to this by breaking all of the Marches' glassware against the wall, which is what made the neighbor call us in the first place.

"Anyway, we wind up driving Hammett back to his hotel, because he couldn't drive himself, and the woman who was with him, Lillian somebody, didn't want to leave the party.

"He starts telling us about his days as a Pink. And that leads to him jawing about the Falcon, and the Skull of Lhasa. He talks about this Midget Bandit, who's in the Falcon under the name of Wilmer, and the Midget's partner, a wild man that Hammett swears he's going to use in a book some day. And he laughs about the coincidence of the real Wilmer finally getting his hands on the real falcon."

He screwed up his face so that his shovel of a chin almost touched the tip of his nose, then sighed and said, "I got another five years before I retire. Now, me, I don't see myself staying in blue another five years, what with guys on the right on the heavy grab and on the left turning 'em in. Sooner or later, somebody is gonna shoot somebody, and I don't want it to be me. So I got a list of potential tickets to the good life—gems that have never surfaced, missing persons, a couple real bang-bang daddies with prices on their heads. Ever' so often information blows in that strikes me as interesting. So I stick around after hours downtown and check out leads. None of 'em has paid off before. But this one ought to bring the average way up."

"How'd you run across the Midget's partner?"

"I just looked up one afternoon and there he was. Seems he's given up boosting in favor of a new grift, some sorta swami mumbo jumbo. This old Highland Park dowager swore out a complaint and so he got dragged in and booked. He has this beetle juice on his face to make him look Hindu and he's wearing a goddamn turban and he calls himself Sandor the All-Seeing. But according to his prints, he's the Midget's partner, Smiler Foy."

"And nobody asked him about the theft in San Francisco?"

"Nobody knew about it. Except me, of course. And now you."

He started to wet my glass again but I stopped him. "I want to be conscious when I meet the swami."

We both stood. "Any idea how you're going to approach him?" Beaudry asked.

"Head on," I said.

That wasn't in Beaudry's lexicon. He screwed up his face and said, "It's your play to call. But the man is slippery as a greased eel. I blinked my eyes and he was out of the lockup."

"Have you got a better suggestion?"

"Nope. But you don't want to spook him."

"Where do I find him?"

"He's got a crummy little rat trap in Venice. On the canal."

"You didn't brace him, by any chance?"

"Hell, no. Brace him? And tip him that I knew about the

skull? What'd be the sense in that? You know me better than that, shamus."

I did at that. Bracing him would have been too simple, and simplicity was not Beaudry's style. It had cost him countless arrests. Now it was going to cost him twenty-five grand.

There was a green sedan parked in front of my car and a small man perched on my front fender. There was more than enough moonlight for me to see that it was Johnny Horne. He was wearing a dark blue suit so shiny it might have been dipped in brilliantine. His shirt was dark, too, with a cream-colored tie that matched his display handkerchief. A wild rose was stuck in his lapel.

As I opened my car door, I asked, "Catching the night air, Johnny? Or do I get to guess what's on your mind?"

"You going after the dingus now?"

I didn't reply.

"Lemme tag along."

"Why?"

He frowned and took a step to the right and a step to the left, like an anxious chicken. He finally blurted, " 'Cause I need to jaw with you about something."

I slipped behind the wheel and opened the other door for him. He got in eagerly. The engine kicked over and we were off to Venice. He coughed and cleared his throat for a few minutes, then asked, "When I was at Q., did you and, uh, Kay . . . well, you know what I'm asking?"

My eyes went to his coat, which was stretched too tightly across his thin chest to be hiding a gun. Not that anything had happened between me and Kay to make him want to draw down on me. I told him so.

He nodded. "Yeah, that's what I thought," he said. "But I had to ask. My head's all screwed up. Those were five long years and my rhythm's jumbled now that I'm out again. Everything's a little off. It's me. I been imagining things."

I glanced over at him. He was staring out at the road, shaking his head. "Kay's the greatest. She did some things for me, coulda got her in Dutch, maybe even put away. Did 'em to keep me out. And when I screwed up so bad she couldn't pull any more strings, she came up once a week, like clockwork. For all five goddamn years. She's there when I get out and she drives me to a swell place she's bought out in Gray Lake. Painted it fresh for me. Neat as a pin. Got flowers planted all around. Like living in a rainbow." He pointed to the wild rose in his lapel. "This came from our own garden, unnerstand?"

I nodded. But I didn't understand. He sounded like he was ready to unspool on me and I didn't need any distractions. Not if I was going to have to deal with Sandor the All-Seeing. Still, it was interesting to hear about the house and garden. He said suddenly, "I'm not going back on the grift. If you ever hear I'm bouncing checks again, I want you to run me down and shoot me. You hear that, pally. You shoot me."

"Relax, Johnny. Nobody's gonna shoot you," I told him. Which shows you how much I knew about anything.

We glided down Venice Boulevard, over the crest where the ocean breeze dropped the temperature at least ten degrees and puffs of fog passed in front of the headlights like spirit tumbleweeds.

Pretty soon we could see the Venice canals. And smell them. They were built in the early 1900's by a real estate mogul named Kinney who had patterned the town after its Italian namesake. But his dream went up in smoke, literally, in the twenties when his pier burned and the canals filled with slime and the bohemians and oddballs moved in.

Sandor lived not far from where Kinney's version of the doge's palace had once stood. I parked across the canal from his shack on an empty, weedy lot inhabited mainly by mosquitoes. Johnny asked, "What're we doing over here?"

"Trying not to make a hell of a lot of noise," I told him. "I want to get a sense of the place."

Sandor had put up a four-foot chicken wire fence around his property line. Its closest side was about ten feet out into the scum-covered canal. The little plaster square it guarded didn't seem to be worth all the trouble.

There were no lights in the yard area, but a bright glow flooded from the back window. A big man was wandering around inside. He was brown-skinned with long gray hair. He was wearing a black short-sleeve shirt and what appeared to be black trousers. He was gesturing with his hands and shouting angrily. It looked like he was arguing with himself.

Something moved in the yard, but I couldn't see what it was. Maybe a dog. On the canal, several gray shapes bobbed. First, it was an ex-con who liked butterflies. Now I had a con man who kept ducks. Maybe I'd have to get a pet myself, a ferret to walk on sunny afternoons.

I told Johnny to sit tight and wait for me. Then I crossed a footbridge that put me on the other side of the canal, two darkened houses away from Sandor's. I unholstered the .38 and hopped the nearest fence, moving quietly through the sandy soil to the next, slightly higher fence.

I walked along it to the front of the house and crossed a lawn until I was facing Sandor's square, flamingo-colored stucco house. A shade blocked the view through the front picture window.

I tried the far side of the house, following the stepping-stones to the rear of the place until I met up with the chicken wire fence. It was only as high as my waist. I waited for a beat, to see if a dog would sniff me out. When none appeared, I pushed down on the chicken wire and stepped over it easily and silently. I could hear Sandor, inside the house, railing on about the powers of the mind.

In the moonlight I could barely see Johnny standing beside my car across the canal. I waved to him, but he didn't wave back.

I moved closer to Sandor's rear door, which was open a few inches. There were three wooden steps leading to it. My plan was simple. A bit too simple, all things considered. I was going to push through the door, draw down on Sandor, and force him to show me the objet d'art. I got as far as the top step when I was attacked from the rear. A pair of large gray geese took a sudden interest in my ankles and legs. They did not pursue me silently. I was so intent on guarding my flank that I did not hear Sandor until he was at the door, shouting, "Mine enemies I shall smite down."

Damned if he wasn't a man of his word.

Consciousness was a thing with feathers. Flapping near my face. I was lying on my back. Sandor, or someone, had dragged me inside the shack, which was now dark. The goose was not attacking me, merely trying to get out of the closed back door.

The hell with the goose.

Whatever I'd been smote with had raised a knob the size of a gumball on the back of my head. I pressed it, winced, and sat up. My gun was still in my hand. I smelled it, and didn't like the odor.

There was more of it in the room.

The gray goose continued to try to flap through the closed door. I staggered to it, threw the door open, and the goose hopped out without a word of thanks. I leaned against a wall and tried to make the floor settle down.

There was a light switch near my hand and I used it. A red

bulb disclosed a bedroom. That is to say a bed was in it. It was covered with a spread decorated with the signs of the zodiac, a nice touch. The walls had been carelessly painted black and silver.

Sandor the All-Seeing had been caught on his blind side. He lay beside his bed, face down. He'd been shot in the back, twice, and the blood had congealed in a dark pool under him. A .32 was near his body.

There was another corpse in the doorway leading to the rest of the house. Johnny Horne was propped against the jamb. He'd lost his hat and one eye. His head was angled so that the blood had drained away from his face. His mouth was open in astonishment. His once ruddy nose might have been made of clay.

I moved past him into a larger room where a curtain was drawn over a picture window. No more bodies. No geese. No jewel-encrusted skulls. Only furniture draped in black. A long sideboard covered in black velvet contained a glass fortune teller's ball, black and silver candles, and little boxes of powders and foul-smelling vials.

A desk yielded six guns of various calibers, a can of oil, and several little white patches of cloth. Sandor evidently took good care of his weapons.

On a coffee table near a black sofa was an ashtray that had been used as a candle holder. The ashes and butts it contained had been emptied, but a drop of wax had trapped something. A neat square of tinfoil.

According to my wristwatch, I hadn't been out longer than an hour. Two men had been murdered and the stage had been set to make it look like . . . what? Sandor had shot Johnny and I had shot the swami? And done what? Fallen over backward and knocked myself unconscious?

The Venice cops might have bought that. But I didn't feel

like giving them the chance. I'd been lucky enough to have been awakened prematurely by the goose. It was time to see how far that luck would take me.

A police car was pulling up in front of the shack as I let myself out the rear door. I was looking for the geese this time, but they'd wandered off to the side of the fence, drawn by the noise the cops were making.

I moved quickly in the opposite direction, wading into the dark, brackish water of the canal. By the time Sandor's back door opened again, I was standing beside my car, dripping on the running board, shivering, and panting as quietly as I could.

I carefully unlatched the door and eased behind the wheel. Across the canal, a uniformed cop entered the backyard with a drawn gun and a flashlight. When the geese hit him, he discharged his gun. Several times. Lights went on all along the canal. People shouted. Two more cops rushed from the murder house.

I kicked my engine over and backed away from the edge of the canal. I didn't put on my lights until I turned onto Venice Boulevard, a full two miles from the murder scene.

"What's up?" Kay Horne asked. She was standing in her doorway wrapped in a silk robe, squinting at me and yawning. I'd left my wet duds dripping all over the bedroom floor of my apartment.

"Better get some clothes on, Kay. We have to go to Beaudry's."

"Something go wrong?"

"A little snag. We'll discuss it at Beaudry's."

"I . . . Johnny didn't come home tonight. He left right after dinner and he didn't come back. He didn't do anything . . . ?"

"Let's worry about Johnny later," I said.

Another half-hour passed before we arrived at Beaudry's bungalow. Kay's green sedan was collecting dew across the street. She eyed it nervously as she got out of my car. "Johnny's here?" she asked.

"I'd be very surprised," I told her.

I rattled the screen door, then put my knuckle to it. Someone moved inside the house. The porch light went on. The front door opened a crack and Beaudry's head, bad haircut and all, poked out. "Kay?" he asked when he spied her. He opened the door wide.

We both went in fast. Beaudry didn't like my being there. He was in his bathrobe, with bare legs and the straps of a gray undershirt showing. He stared at us. Kay took the sofa. I leaned against the bookcase, while Beaudry closed the front door.

I unbuttoned my coat and said, "Things went a little awry tonight." And with them staring at me attentively, I told them as much as I had observed at Sandor's, before and after I'd been sapped.

When I described in detail the condition of Johnny Horne's head, Kay's blue eyes got their sad look back. But it was an act. I said to them, "What I don't understand is why you crazy kids just didn't run off together. Why put on this goofy Toby show? You always had a weird way of thinking, Beaudry, but jeweled skulls! Jesus!"

"There is one," Beaudry said angrily. "All that stuff is true."

"It's just that Sandor didn't happen to have it."

Beaudry shook his head. "Naw. It belonged to one of Hammett's Pinkerton pals. Far as Hammett knew, the guy still had it."

"How was it supposed to go down?" I asked.

"You figure it out, shamus. You're the bright boy."

Beaudry was moving away from Kay. I didn't like that, so I edged toward him, keeping them both in sight.

"You and Kay have been playing house for a while. Long enough for her to tidy up this place and fill the tables with flowers from her garden. The only things in the beds outside are weeds."

I turned to her. "I guess you couldn't spruce up the grounds too much, what with nosy neighbors and all."

"We can work on the garden later," Beaudry said, as if he meant it.

"Not after they hang two murders on you," I told him.

Kay sighed and reached into her coat pocket. I tensed, but it was a cigarette she was after. She lighted up and said, "It seemed like a good idea at the time."

"How'd you get Johnny out here tonight?"

She said wearily, "He was getting wise that I was . . . interested in somebody, so I sort of hinted that it was you. I was hoping he'd follow you to the swami's. He did even better: He talked you into letting him come along."

I turned to Beaudry. "And Sandor was primed for our visit, right? Judging by his arsenal, the swami was also a hired shooter. You paid him to put the slug on me and take out Johnny. I'd wake up, see that Sandor had flown, and assume that he'd bumped off Johnny because of the jeweled doodad. Only something went wrong. What was it, Kay? I know you were there. I saw the neat little square you tear from your cigarette packs. What was it that Sandor wanted? More money?"

"He wanted to kill you, too," Kay said flatly. "Said it would be cleaner. He had his pistol pressed against your temple when I picked up your gun and shot him."

I didn't know if I wanted to believe her or not. I said, "Was that before or after he shot Johnny?"

"Johnny was already dead," she said and looked away.

"Johnny wouldn't have just walked in there. But he would have come running if you'd called to him."

She said nothing.

I continued, "He told me you'd done some things to help him out, things that might have put you in trouble with the cops. Maybe you played around with some evidence, misfiled a few papers. Was that what you were afraid of, that he'd spill if you ditched him for Beaudry and you'd wind up in the slammer?"

"Something like that," she said and took more smoke into her lungs.

Beaudry said, "What the hell good will it do to put Kay through the wringer on this, Marlowe? You know damn well Johnny was no great loss."

"He liked butterflies," I told him. "Besides, maybe Sandor didn't kill Johnny."

"You can't think that Kay . . ."

"You mean an ex-cop wouldn't dream of using a gun on a husband she wanted dead? Actually, Beaudry, I was thinking that this is your kind of play. Too complicated by half. Maybe you followed us there tonight and pulled the trigger yourself."

He dug his hand deeper into his robe pocket. He said, "I never been near the place."

I bent down and picked up something from the polished floor. A gray goose feather.

I saw his arm tense and pushed myself away from the wall of books, drawing my gun as I went. His robe pocket exploded and a bullet tore the hide off of a book on the shelf. He paused too long to stare at the ruined book and I shot him several times in the chest. The force of the slugs lifted him off his feet and knocked him back into the door he had just closed.

Kay gave a sharp scream and ran to him.

She didn't cry.

By the time the cops arrived, she was cradling Beaudry's ugly, lifeless head in her lap, but she still hadn't cried. She had the saddest eyes I'd ever seen, but she didn't seem to have a tear to put in them.

I never found out if she'd really saved my life in Sandor's shack. But I did finally discover, quite by accident, what Beaudry had been trying to tell me in Harold Wilde's office the day I was fired. On a surveillance job that kept me holed up in the Bay City library for six days, I happened to open a book of poems by the guy who wrote *Gulliver's Travels*, Jonathan Swift, and read: "So, naturalists observe, a flea/ hath smaller fleas that on him prey;/ And these have smaller still to bite 'em;/ And so proceed ad infinitum."

Some reader, that Beaudry. But he should have stuck with Swift and stayed clear of Hammett.

Vampire Dreams

"We're back in business at last, eh, Byron," Simon Winklas said with a grin. He was a dapper little man with a polished bald head and large, tinted eyeglasses.

Byron Ruthven smiled and sipped his icy martini. His lazy, pale blue eyes swept the restaurant in which he and Simon were prominently seated. One of Hollywood's palaces of power, it was packed to its palm fronds with film people—stars, would-be stars, somber-suited moneymen who would be picking up the tabs, and the occasional tourist being escorted by the surly maitre d' to a far corner that used to be called Siberia before the advent of Glasnost. Now it was called Bakersfield.

Ruthven consulted his wristwatch and asked the tiny man, "If they want me so badly, Simon, why are they so late?"

"You've been in this business for at least forty years that I've known you, Byron. You ever hear of a producer getting to a dinner meeting early?"

"Sam Spiegel."

"Sam was a gentleman. Frank Lorenzo is . . . well, Frank Lorenzo."

"Do you know how the Lorenzos made their money, Simon?" Ruthven asked, taking another sip of his martini.

"Mafia?" Simon whispered.

Ruthven laughed. "No, but the Mafia probably threw some business their way. They were morticians. Frank gave all that up to get into the movies."

"No wonder he produces so many stiffs," Simon said,

chuckling. Then he grew suddenly serious as a group of people headed their way. "O.K. They're here. Be nice."

"I'm always nice," Ruthven said, rising to his full six-foot-three as a quintet of people arrived at his table.

The maitre d' frowned and said, "I'm sorry. I was told a table for six. But if you don't mind crowding . . ."

"We do," Frank Lorenzo said flatly. He was a large, deeply tanned man wearing a suit of appropriate brown sharkskin. His voice was a slurred, guttural growl. "Th' bloodsucker," he gestured with his chin toward Simon, "can go buy his own dinner."

"I suppose we both can," Ruthven said.

"No. I wanna talk with you. We don't need him."

Assuming that his word was final, Lorenzo sat down across from Ruthven and tucked his napkin into the open neck of his silk shirt. Slowly, the other members of his party took their chairs also, familiar with, if not approving of, their host's rudeness.

Simon tried to make the best of it. "We can talk later, Byron," he said, backing away from the table like a scolded cur. Ruthven opened his mouth in protest, but Simon shook his head. Ruthven was independently wealthy and did not need the work, but he realized that Simon was relying heavily on his ten percent.

"Sit!" Lorenzo ordered and Ruthven sat. "You know these folks, Byron? This," he clutched the thin arm of the young man next to him, "this is my genius-boy, Dennis Murch, the best goddamn director in this burg. *Time* magazine said he 'finds more horror in suburbia than Poe found in the back alleys of Paris.' "

Ruthven had heard about Murch, of course. He'd even rented videocassettes of two of the young man's recent films. They were amusing, but he found them more perverse than frightening. Of course, it took quite a lot to frighten him.

"And he's all mine for his next three pictures," Lorenzo went on. He gestured to a bookish fellow to his right. "The fat, sleepy-looking bastid is Thad Hatten, who's got some real beauty sets and special effects that'll knock your eyes out. This ain't like the old days, Byron, when we had cardboard bats on strings." He reached into his pocket and produced a set of plastic teeth. "Look at this, bubby." Lorenzo pressed a bump on the plastic gum and the two eye teeth began to grow. "How's about that?"

"Fascinating," Ruthven said. "And who are these toothsome ladies?"

"My name is Noreen Bailey, Mr. Ruthven," said the small blonde to his left. "I'm Dennis's fiancée."

"And on your right," Lorenzo growled, "is the woman responsible for our meeting tonight, Emma Lomax, author of *Vampire Dreams*."

Emma Lomax was a stunning brunette in, Ruthven imagined, her early thirties. She was willowy and languidly graceful, with dark green eyes that reminded him of eyes he had once caused to fill with tears in what seemed like another lifetime.

She stared at him, then said, "It's amazing. You look exactly like you did in 'Dracula Must Be Destroyed,' and that was what? thirty years ago?"

"It's all a matter of attitude and a little makeup," Ruthven said. "I enjoyed your book immensely."

"What about the script?" Lorenzo demanded.

Ruthven stared at him for a beat, then said, "Very interesting."

"What didn't you like?"

"Most of the modern stuff that wasn't in the book. The AIDS business . . ."

Emma Lomax smiled triumphantly and turned to Lorenzo. "Don't say it," he commanded her. "The AIDS touch was mine, Byron. I want this film to be contemporary. This is an 'A' film, not one of those bite-the-neck exploitation flicks we useta churn out. The AIDS stuff is for the good of the movie. I know what I'm saying."

"It's using a plague to sell a mass-market movie," Ruthven said.

"You're gonna make me sorry I insisted we hire you, Byron," Lorenzo said. "Dennis kept pushing for somebody like Newman, or even Eastwood for the father vampire. But I said it had to be my old star, Byron Ruthven. And now you're pimping me about the script."

Dennis Murch cleared his throat and said, "I didn't say I didn't want you, Mr. Ruthven. It's just that I assumed you had retired from film."

"I had."

Lorenzo said, "For no good reason that I could see. Our Dracula movies were making classic money. We coulda milked the monster for at least a half-dozen more, but Byron the dilettante decided to go into mourning for a dame he barely knew."

"That's enough," Ruthven said quietly but firmly.

"Well, it was a blessing in disguise for me, anyway," Lorenzo said. "It forced me into movin' up in class. I owe my success to Byron here, which is the main reason I wanted to give him a shot in 'Vampire Dreams.' "

"You want me because Newman and Eastwood get millions and I don't," Ruthven said.

"There's nothing wrong with that! More of the budget will wind up on the screen. It's for the good of the picture."

"Shouldn't we order some food?" Noreen Bailey suggested.

"In a minute," Lorenzo snapped, staring at Ruthven. "Are you in or out?"

"I'm here, putting up with your rudeness," Ruthven said.

"You're a goddamn dilettante who don't need the money. You never did. If you don't like the script, why do the movie?"

"Because of Miss Lomax's wonderful novel," Ruthven said. "With any luck, and a bit of skill, it should make an excellent film."

"Then we got a deal?"

"We could iron out all the details right now," Ruthven said, "if my agent were here."

For the rest of the dinner, Lorenzo held sway. While he presented his views on wine, the state of the economy, the inanity of most new films, the ingratitude of actors and the capriciousness of the movie going public, Ruthven picked at his food and studied Emma Lomax's profile. Every so often, her dark green eyes would turn his way and he would hold them with his own for a few moments before smiling and breaking the contact. Finally, he leaned close to her and whispered something in her ear.

It was nearing eleven when the parking attendant retrieved Ruthven's Jaguar convertible; the actor opened the passenger door for Emma Lomax.

"Hey," Lorenzo growled, "she came with me."

"Byron suggested we discuss the script a bit," Emma said.

"It's for the good of the movie, Frank," Ruthven said as he slid behind the wheel.

As they drove away from the scowling Lorenzo, Emma gave him her address. Then she said, "Nothing we do will make Frank change the script, you know."

"Actually, I didn't want to talk about the script at all. I wanted to talk about your book."

"Oh?"

"You made several interesting departures from Mr. Stoker's immortal tome," he said as the car drove smoothly through the warm Southern California night. "The business about the vampire's adaptability, for example. The idea that, just as the flesh eating human might, for the sake of his health, became a vegetarian, the vampire might wean himself from blood and onto something equally nutritional, like consommé or broth. A brilliant notion."

She smiled. "It's not original. It was my grandfather's idea. He used to tell me such wonderful stories about vampires when I was a child."

"Was your grandfather's name Lomax, too?"

"No. He was my maternal grandparent. His name was Marcus Van Helsing."

"Ah," Ruthven exclaimed. "I thought there was something . . . Your mother was Lucy Van Helsing."

She nodded.

"You have her eyes," he said.

"You know my mother?"

"Your grandfather was one of the genuine experts in the field of vampirism. I talked Frank into hiring him as consultant on our first films. Some days, your mother would accompany him to the set." He was skirting the truth. He had known Lucy Van Helsing quite well. He had known Emma's great-grandfather Abraham, too, but there was no need to get into that with her, either.

"Mother and dad live in Europe. In Germany."

"I think I'd heard that," he said. "Though I don't recall knowing her married name."

"I'll have to tell her we're working together."

"She'll be quite amused, I expect," Ruthven said.

The Jaguar turned into a cul-de-sac that seemed to be cut into the side of a hill. Ruthven parked beside an outdoor elevator designed to carry its occupants to the top of the hill where a maze of apartments had been constructed like an eccentric beehive.

He accompanied her on the trip up. At her door, she turned, waited for a beat, then asked, "You kept staring at me all through dinner. I felt . . ."

"Felt what?" he asked.

"That we've known one another for a long time."

"Old souls," he said, smiling.

She asked, "Would you like to kiss me?"

"Very much so," he said, but made no move to do so.

"Well, then?"

When he didn't reply, she said, "Please don't worry about the difference in our ages. I'm very drawn to you. I'd like us to be . . . good friends."

"We'll see," he said. He took her hand and kissed it. Its proximity made him slightly dizzy with desire. It had been years since he had felt that familiar longing. To withstand it, he had to give up her mother. He said, "We'll see soon enough, I fear."

In the weeks that followed, Emma visited the filming of "Vampire Dreams" almost every day, but was dismayed to discover that Ruthven seemed to be avoiding her. Actually, he was avoiding everyone. Dennis Murch was annoyed that Ruthven made himself available only at night for working out scenes with the moody Brandoesque stage actor who was playing his son.

"He's always been like that," Frank Lorenzo explained. "Something about his metabolism. He's a night person. During the day, he needs lots of rest breaks. It's in his contract. If the cameras aren't rolling, then he stays in his trailer." The latter was a Winnebago dressing room with dark tinted windows that was parked not far from the sets, inside the huge soundstage.

Those were difficult days for Emma. She hated herself for behaving like an infatuated schoolgirl, trying to gain just a glimpse of her dream lover. One evening, she waited near Ruthven's Jaguar for nearly two hours, but he didn't leave the soundstage. The next morning, she arrived practically at dawn, but the Jaguar was already there. It made her suspect that he was using the Winnebago as a temporary home.

One day she asked Frank Lorenzo, "Why did Byron stop acting?"

The producer raised an eyebrow. "Why do you wanna know?"

"Just curious."

"Well, don't get too curious. And don't bother 'im. I say this for the good of the movie. I don't want anything on Byron's mind but 'Vampire Dreams.' "

It was the director's fiancée, Noreen Bailey, who told her about the woman named Jeanette Bouvan, a costume designer on Ruthven's last picture, "A Bride For Dracula." "This was, like, twenty-five years ago. Evidently, Byron Ruthven and the Bouvan woman met on the picture and, well, did the thing. According to this book I read, *Hollywood Horrorshow*, which tells about all the murders and weird stuff that's ever happened out here, the Bouvan woman disappeared one night. Ruthven went a little wacko. And then when they found her body, he went totally bananas."

"Found her body?"

"Yes," Noreen said, breathily. "In one of the canyons, naked and mutilated. She'd been sexually assaulted before she was murdered. But that's not all. The really weird thing is that she had these holes in her neck and all the blood had been drained from her body. The papers called it 'The Vampire Murder.' "

"That took a lot of imagination," Emma said. "Who killed her?"

"Well, that's the thing," Noreen answered. "They never found the murderer. It's like the Black Dahlia and all the rest. Anyway, Byron Ruthven, who'd made a career of playing Dracula, sort of hung up his cape because of it. Nobody actually accused him of killing the woman, but, I mean, come on. Here he was in the movie biting women on the neck and drinking their blood, and his girlfriend gets murdered in that weird way. Anyway, there was all this hullabaloo. And Ruthven went into seclusion."

"That's a ghastly story," Emma said.

The next day she bought a copy of *Hollywood Horrorshow*, but there was not much in the book that had been missing from Noreen's synopsis. Just the fact that the murder had made "A Bride for Dracula" one of the surprise hits of the year.

She began Xeroxing newspaper stories about the murder, bringing them to the desk allotted her in the production office. After working out the changes to the script that were requested on an almost daily basis, she would try to assemble the facts surrounding the death of Jeanette Bouvan.

She was scanning an article from a sixties magazine called *Scandal* when Frank Lorenzo bulled into the office, followed by Dennis Murch.

Murch was complaining, "Frank, we've got these two vampires, father and son, living in a small town. The whole point is that they're fitting in. The townspeople like them. The whole movie is about the horror that exists even in the most normal surroundings. How in heaven's name can we shoehorn a dormitory shower scene into this?"

"Maybe the old vampire takes his son out for a fly around

the campus. I dunno. I'm not creative, I admit. All I know is that kids love to see wet, naked babes. And kids buy the tickets." He put his arm around Murch's thin back and led him to the door. "Trust me. It's for the good of the movie."

Lorenzo closed the office door on Murch's protesting face, turned, sighed and spotted Emma at her desk. "What's 'at you got?" he asked, taking the article from her hand.

" 'Jeanette Bouvan, a victim of the undead,' " he read with scorn. "Geeze, Emma, don't you have enough to do with the script and your next book."

"This may be my next book," she said.

"The twenty-five-year-old murder of some bimbo? What's such a big deal about that?"

"The question is: how did the blood get drawn from her body?"

He chuckled. "A vampire, like the papers said."

"You don't believe in vampires?" It was almost an accusation. He shrugged, tossed the article back onto her desk and headed for his private office. "They made me a fortune. Sure I believe in 'em." His voice was heavy with sarcasm, "Just like I believe in net profits."

She said, "If there are no vampires, then why was the body bloodless?"

He paused, then grinned at her. "I got a theory about that," he said, "which I will be glad to discuss over dinner tonight. You interested?"

She'd been turning down his invitations since she met him. But this was one she couldn't refuse.

It was shortly after two A.M. when Ruthven heard the banging on his Winnebago door. He threw on a robe and opened the door to a terrified and wounded Emma Lomax.

He helped her to a sofa and attempted to calm her. ". . . tried to . . . ," she got out.

"Who?" he asked, staring at the scratches on her face and arms and legs, the torn dress.

"I . . . think I killed him."

"Who?"

"Frank. I . . . hit him and hit him and killed him."

He held her to him and she began sobbing. He said, "I'll take care of it."

"But I killed him," she said. "Or I think I did."

"We'll see."

He carried her to the bed, covered her with a down comforter. He forced her to take a sedative from the medicine cabinet, then said, "Tell me what happened."

"I've been collecting material on the murder of Jeanette Bouvan," she said, studying his face for some sign. Seeing none, she went on. "Frank said he had an idea about the murder and he'd tell me about it over dinner. I didn't know he meant at his apartment. His manservant prepared the food, then Frank told him to go away, that we wanted to be alone. I still didn't get it. I thought he wanted privacy to tell me something special about the murder. But all he wanted was to . . ."

"Did he say anything about Jeanette?"

She hesitated. "He said he thought you had killed her."

"Oh?"

"I asked him why and he said that maybe you were a vampire."

Ruthven said, "I didn't think Frank was the sort to believe in vampires."

"He's not." Her eyelids were fluttering. The sedative was doing its job. Yawning, she continued, "He said that the only real vampires are the ones you find in the back rooms of mortuaries."

Ruthven's pale blue eyes widened in surprise. How could he have overlooked something as obvious as that? He pulled the comforter up around her neck. "Sleep," he said softly. "When you wake up, this whole night will be nothing more than a dream."

She started to protest. His eyes held hers. "Just a dream. You dined with Frank. You discussed the script. When you left, Frank was making plans to meet another woman."

". . . another woman," she said, half-asleep.

He passed a long thin hand over her eyes and closed them.

The door to Frank Lorenzo's penthouse was ajar.

Ruthven found him in the living room on the floor, his forehead bloody from a gash in his scalp. The objet d'art responsible, a Golden Globe Award, rested on the carpet beside him.

The smell of blood was fresh in Ruthven's nostrils as he pressed his fingertips to Lorenzo's neck, felt a pulse. He slapped the big man's face and Lorenzo sputtered to life. "Wha' the hell?"

He winced. His large hand went to his head and came away red. "Damnit! Where is she?"

"Gone," Ruthven said simply.

"Where'd you come from, Byron?" The big man grunted as he rose to his feet, swayed and staggered into another room and switched on the light. Ruthven followed.

It was a master bedroom, black silks covering the bed, mirrors covering one wall. Lorenzo paused before the mirrored wall, examining his scalp. "Damn, she banged me up pretty good. When I get my hands on that bit . . ."

"You won't," Ruthven said.

Lorenzo's eyes tried to find Ruthven in the mirror, but he couldn't. He blinked, then spun round. The tall actor was only a few feet away from him, and Lorenzo jumped. "Geeze,

Byron, you're spookin' me."

"Do you have any idea who I am, Frank?"

Lorenzo glared at him for a second, then said, "Yeah, you're an over-the-hill actor trying to be funny. My head's killin' me. I gotta get a Percodan." He staggered through a door.

Ruthven followed him and when Lorenzo started to pry the cap off a prescription bottle, slapped the bottle from the producer's hand.

Lorenzo scowled at Ruthven, a storm gathering on his bloody face. Ruthven said, "I don't want any drugs in your bloodstream."

"You don't want? Who gives a damn what you want?"

"Do you know where the name Ruthven comes from, Frank?"

"Name?" Lorenzo's forehead was wrinkled now, in confusion. "I dunno. Your old man?"

Ruthven laughed. "Do you recall how Mary Shelley was inspired to write Frankenstein during a weekend she spent with her husband and Lord Byron?"

Lorenzo looked at him dumbly. "I saw the movie," he said. "It was supposed to be sexy but it was a stinker."

"There was another member of that party, a Dr. John Polidori. At the same time that Mary Shelley was concocting her infamous monster, the good doctor was working on his."

"I don't know what the hell you're talking about," Lorenzo moaned. "I just know my head hurts."

"Dr. Polidori wrote a novella titled 'The Vampyre,' about a rather nefarious fellow named Ruthven. The story was well received. A number of critics thought that Byron had written it."

"So your name's Ruthven, too. So big deal."

"You don't understand," Ruthven said. "Dr. Polidori gave me my name."

"Huh?"

109

"Since then, I've been given other names. The penny dreadfuls called me Lord Varney. Horrible writing. Just like your movies. Then another author saw me on the London stage, appearing as Lucifer, and when he wrote about me, he called me Dracula."

"Right," Lorenzo said, patronizingly. "Nice meeting ya, Mr. Dracula." Then he mumbled, "Goddamn fruitcake."

"When I decided to settle on the West Coast, the name Dracula was so well-known and feared, I selected the less-famous one provided by Dr. Polidori."

Lorenzo wasn't sure if Ruthven had gone totally loony or if this was some sort of actor's prank. Either way, what did it matter? "That's a good story," he said. "Save it for Leno." He stooped to pick up the pill bottle.

Ruthven quickly entered the bathroom and stepped on the bottle, crushing it and the pills it contained.

"O. K. That's enough . . . !" Lorenzo stared up at him, straightened and charged at the actor.

Ruthven took two quick steps backward and Lorenzo stumbled into the bedroom, a bull galloping past the matador. He regained his balance and moved slowly toward Ruthven. He placed a large hand on the actor's thin chest and with a snarl pushed with all his strength. But Ruthven did not budge. He was as immovable as a cast-iron statue.

Lorenzo felt a sudden chill. "Get the hell out of here!" he shouted.

"Not until I take care of something I should have a long time ago."

"You're makin' me goddamn mad. Get out while you can," Lorenzo warned.

"Not just yet," Ruthven said. Suddenly, his fist struck Lorenzo just below the rib cage. It was a powerful punch. The big man buckled and fell to the floor.

Lorenzo tried to push himself upright, but Ruthven kicked his arm out from under him. "Why're you doing this?" the big man yelled, panting on the floor.

"I always thought you killed Jeanette," Ruthven said. "I just didn't know how you got rid of her blood. I even began to wonder if you might be a vampire. But as the years passed I decided it didn't much matter. She was gone. I might have saved her, given her life, but the cost would have been too great, to her and to me."

"You're one crazy bastid."

"You told Emma that the only vampires were the ones found in the back rooms of mortuaries. That's where they drain the blood, isn't it, before injecting the formaldehyde? That's what you did with Jeanette, isn't it, Frank? You raped her and killed her and took her over to the family mortuary and drew off her blood."

Lorenzo crawled away from him, backwards, until he reached a wall. He used it to stand. "Keep away from me, you nut case."

"You call *me* a nut case. You, who forced yourself upon a woman, murdered her and then desecrated her body."

Lorenzo yanked open the drawer to a night table beside the bed. There was a pistol in the drawer and he pointed it at Ruthven. It gave him a certain confidence. "I didn't mean to kill her, Byron," he said. "It was sort of a misunderstanding. I was playin' a little rough and it was like she . . . broke. So there I was. Nothing I could do would bring her back, so I figured, as long as she was dead, why not use it? The movie was about to be released. Why not make the papers start talking about vampires?"

"I have known an infinite amount of diseased monsters in my time," Ruthven said, "but you are the last curly kink of the demon's tail."

"And you're a dead man," Lorenzo said, pulling the trigger.

"Wrong on both counts," Ruthven said as the bullets lodged in his chest.

Lorenzo waited for Ruthven to fall, but he didn't. He took several steps across the room. Lorenzo's gun roared again. Again, the bullets found their mark. Then the big man felt the gun being twisted from his grasp. Ruthven opened his mouth and his canine teeth began to grow.

"These are not special effects, Frank," Ruthven told him. "They're the real thing."

They clamped onto Lorenzo's neck.

Lorenzo felt an electric shock, then a sense of profound peace. Slowly, as the blood was withdrawn from his body, he began to sink into a cloudy fog that darkened until he felt nothing at all.

Ruthven moved swiftly through the penthouse, tidying up, wiping Emma's fingerprints from the globular statue and replacing it on a table. Then he lifted the big man easily and carried him out onto the balcony. He stared down seventeen stories to the cement drive. The fall would cover a multitude of contusions and abrasions. And by the time the body landed, Ruthven's wings would have taken him miles from the scene.

He balanced the body on the balcony rail. "Your blood was probably tainted," he told the dead man, "and it will take me years to return to a less sanguinary diet. Addictions are so hard to break. But, as you proved with poor Jeanette's corpse, a bit of real-life vampirism does sell movie tickets.

"You should appreciate this, Frank," he said, as the bloodless body plummeted downward. "It's for the good of the movie."

A Tough Case to Figure

The big man seated across the desk from me obviously had experienced trouble firsthand. He was wearing a plaster on his forehead the size of a credit card. His left eye was swollen and his mouth had a puffy, worked-over look.

He was taking the long way around to tell me how it all happened. ". . . then the woman—she said her name was Alice—she grabbed my hand and led me out of the place."

"Place got a name?" I asked.

"Laroque's House of Heaven," he said.

"A bar."

"Sort of. It's in the French Quarter."

"I don't suppose there's more than one Laroque's," I said. "It's definitely a bar."

"But I hadn't had very much to drink."

I cocked a skeptical eyebrow at him.

"No, really," he said, defensively. "Two scotches, tops. I'm not a drinking man. Really."

"Nobody who visits New Orleans is a drinking man, Mr. Benham," I told him. "Or a man who plays around. It's something in the air."

His frown told me he didn't like my attitude. "I came for help, not a discussion of my morals."

I didn't reply, just stared at him, waiting for him to get around to the help part. He'd been in my office for nearly fifteen minutes and he'd given up very little. His name was Leland Edgar Benham, of the Virginia Benhams. He was staying at the home of a local master of medicine named Paul LeBlanc, who had hired my agency a few months back to retrieve his wandering daughter. We, my partner Joe Mallory and I, found her in Gulfport, Mississippi, living in a condo with a young guy named Esteban. Since they had gone to the effort of legalizing their union, and since she was of age, that was that for the LeBlanc case. Doc LeBlanc may not have been entirely satisfied with the outcome, but we'd done our work quickly and with discretion. Which I assumed was what impressed him enough to send more business our way.

Benham pulled back his sleeve and glanced nervously at a gold Rolex on his wrist.

"Keeping you from something, Mr. Benham?" I asked.

"Sorry," he snapped, nervously. "I'm anxious to get back to the LeBlanc house. Give my bruises a rest."

"Sure," I said. "So you were leaving the bar with a lady named Alice . . ."

"Right. We left the bar. A block away, three guys wearing stocking masks pushed us into an alley. They wanted my money. When I didn't give it to them fast enough, they started hitting me."

"What about Alice?"

He made a helpless gesture with his hands. "I think she got away. I don't know for sure. I was pretty busy."

"Even with three of 'em, they were taking a chance," I said, surveying his size and shape.

"I got a punch or two in."

I pointed to his scraped and raw knuckles. "Maybe more than two?"

"I did what I could. But it wasn't enough. They did a job on me. Then they snatched my wallet and took off. I crawled out of the alley and somehow made it back to the car I'd bor-

114

rowed from Paul LeBlanc. Paul patched me up himself."

"The best healing hands in the business," I said. "I suppose you reported the mugging to the cops?"

He hesitated, then said, "What's the point? They won't spend much time on a simple French Quarter mugging."

"And you probably wouldn't want to go on record about your hitting the bars with little Alice."

"No. I wouldn't," he said.

"Married man?" I asked, my eyes dropping to the naked fingers of his battered left hand.

"Not yet. Engaged. I don't want to make a big thing of this. I understood you were discreet."

"Discretion is our byword," I told him. "Won't the fiancée be curious about the bruises?"

"I'll be traveling for the next three weeks. Let's see how I look then."

"Well, Mr. Benham, what exactly do you want?" I asked. "Revenge? Your money back? What?"

"I'm not interested in revenge or the money. It was only a couple hundred dollars. I've canceled the credit cards. But there were other things, credentials, that I'd like to recover. What are my chances?"

I told him I thought we might just turn up something. Then we discussed the money thing and cut a deal.

As soon as he'd hobbled out of the office, I rattled Mallory's cage next door and sent him to keep an eye on Benham. Guys who get mugged in the Quarter don't usually hold on to their gold watches. Maybe he'd been lucky and maybe something else was going on.

I got out the phone book and dialed Laroque's House of Heaven. Alice was such a regular that even the day barkeep knew her. Alice Russo. Apartment on Camp Street in the low-rent district.

★ ★ ★ ★ ★

She was tall and large-boned. A little high-strung. Not bad, if you don't mind the boyish look, which I don't. She seemed afraid of me, which made the job easier. After we'd had our little chat, I put in a call to Benham and set up another meeting.

Mallory was in his car, parked down the street from the LeBlanc home in the Garden District. "Our man come straight here from the office?" I asked him.

Mallory nodded, then scowled at me. "You look worried. Something wrong?" he asked.

"I don't know," I told him. "It's a tough case to figure. Let's go see if we can simple it up a little."

Mallory patted the gun holstered under his jacket. It seemed to give him confidence.

Dr. Paul LeBlanc let us in. He was a little olive-skinned guy with a thin moustache who didn't look like he'd know beans about gray matter. But the word was, if something went wrong up there, he was the knife man you wanted to dig in and set it right. He said Benham was waiting for us in the solarium. The last time I'd seen LeBlanc, when I'd told him about his daughter getting hitched to her Latino lover, there'd been nothing shy about him. But just then, he wasn't looking me in the eye.

I put on the brakes and slapped my forehead. "I'm a jackass," I told him. "Is it four o'clock yet?"

"Nearly that," the doctor said.

"Aww. The time got away from me. We're supposed to be clear across town right now."

"But, I thought—" Doc LeBlanc began.

"We'll be back in an hour," I told him, giving Mallory the "out of here" sign with my thumb.

As we started for the door, Benham joined the party from the solarium. "You're not going?" he asked. He draped a heavy

116

arm over my shoulders. It was a friendly enough gesture.

"Mr. Mallory and I have something urgent to attend to," I said. "We'll be back—"

"As long as you're here," Benham said, steering me toward the solarium, "why not take a minute and get our business settled?"

The little doc excused himself and left us. Mallory, even more confused than usual, trailed Benham and me into the solarium. The afternoon sun was still bright and the glass room was warm. We sat on wicker chairs beside a row of green and blue and yellow flowers, me facing Benham and Mallory. Mallory's eyebrows were raised so high they were almost touching his toupee.

"You said on the phone you'd made progress," Benham told me. "You found my wallet?"

"No. But I found Alice."

"Oh." He sounded disappointed. "She all right?"

"She looked fine."

"Was she in it with them? Did she set me up?"

The guy seemed so damned sincere, and his bruises were the real thing. I decided I was getting spooked over nothing. "No. She's a victim like you. And . . . she's got this problem."

"Problem?"

"The muggers have threatened her," I said.

"I don't understand."

We'd arrived at the trickiest part. Alice had been a little vague about what happened after the mugging. "When they took care of you," I said, "they slapped her around a little and scared the hell out of her."

"The bastards," Benham spat out. "Does she know who they are?"

"No. But they know her and they know where she lives. And she's afraid."

"The poor kid," Benham said, obviously concerned.

"Yeah. Well, the poor kid is about to go to the cops for protection."

Benham stared at me blankly. Not getting it. I had to spell it out for him. "She's gonna go to the cops, Mr. Benham. That means the cops will want to talk with you. And they'll want to know why you didn't go to them earlier. And maybe the *Times-Picayune* stringer who hangs around the NOPD will get interested and you'll wind up with a lot of free newspaper publicity you don't want."

"I can't have that happen," he said.

"Then it may cost you a little money."

"Money? For what?" Denham asked.

"Alice says she either goes to the law or she splits from New Orleans," I told him. "Only she doesn't have the cash for a trip."

"How much does she need?"

"She says two thousand should get her to relatives in Atlanta."

"Two thousand dollars?" Denham squealed. I shrugged and waited for him to mull it over.

"You think I should pay her?" he asked.

"Either that, or she has to go to the cops, dragging you along."

"Can't you find the men and put them away?" He sounded really desperate.

"Putting 'em away will drag you into it, too," I said. "It's much cleaner if she clears out."

"Hell," he said. "I suppose I can get the cash. Then what? Do I take it to her?"

"Don't worry about that," I told him. "We can handle that part of it."

"I bet you can," he said, grinning suddenly.

The grin sent a chill up my spine. I looked at Mallory. His hand was edging toward his right lapel.

"What if I told you," the big guy said, "that my name isn't Benham and I don't come from Virginia and my face and hands look like this because I ran into a couple of smart guys who were running the badger game in L.A.? As bad as I look, they look worse. And they're being treated by prison doctors."

"You're not the law," I said. "What's your game?"

"My name's Bloodworth. I'm a P.I. from Los Angeles. The Manion Detective Agency sent for me because I'm not known here. We wrote the scenario to fit my bruises and contusions."

The room was too hot. I could feel the sweat dripping down the back of my neck. Bloodworth was facing me. To his right, Mallory waited for some sign.

"The LeBlancs hired Manion, huh?" I asked.

"Just as soon as they found out you'd extorted money from Julio Esteban to keep quiet until after he'd married their daughter."

"That's crap," I said. "That never happened."

"It would have been your word against Esteban's. Which is why Manion and I had to stage this dog and pony show."

"It's entrapment."

"No entrapment," the big guy said. "We'll even give your lawyer a copy of the transcript of our conversation, let him go over every line."

I scowled at him. "A couple of bucks. I'll be out in a year. Six months."

"That's all we were going for," Bloodworth said. "In spite of yourself, you did the LeBlancs and the Estebans a good turn. They're all one big happy family now. United in the desire to teach you a lesson. Just a little lesson.

"But you had to get rough with Alice. She's a friend of mine. And you'll pay for that with a few more years. Both you and your monkey."

It was definitely time to give Mallory the sign and he dragged his gun clear of his coat. With surprising speed, Bloodworth shifted his body and hit Mallory in the face, busting his nose and sending him and his chair over backwards.

Then the big man was on his feet, plucking Mallory's gun from the floor and slipping it into his pocket.

He moved toward me and I raised my hands, showing they were empty. Flat on the deck, Mallory moaned, more unconscious than not.

"I ought to pound you, too," Bloodworth said, "for slapping Alice around."

"Tell her I enjoyed it," I said.

Dr. LeBlanc came to the door of the solarium to announce that the police were on their way. With him was a thin guy with glasses. I'd seen him around. Manion. "Good work, Leo," he said to Bloodworth.

"Good work? Wearing that Rolex was bush league," I told Bloodworth, trying to make his victory a little less sweet.

"It was dumb," he admitted. "We were lucky that greed made you dumber."

After that, I waited for the cops in silence.

Get the Message

"I can tell you this, Manion. The man's a duplicitous weevil or my name isn't Samuel Belladorn."

The prospective client sitting on the other side of my desk wrapped his name in such a thick coating of pride I lifted my eyes from my twirling thumbs for another look at him. His rounded body was still squeezed tight in the client chair and his ruddy, raw face, with its protruding eyes and thin twitching mouth, was every bit as beautiful as when he'd walked into my office ten minutes before.

"What exactly can I do for you, Mr. Belladorn? Weevils may be a bit out of my line. I'm an investigator, not an exterminator."

He cocked his head to one side and stared at me, like a chicken pondering the nutritional content of an unfamiliar wiggle-worm. "That's a kinda sarcastic tone for a working man to take, isn't it?"

"Well, I'm a sarcastic sort of working man," I told him. "But I get the work done. Assuming I ever find out what it is."

He wrinkled his nose in obvious distaste, then put his head back on straight. "My sister is a very, ah, innocent woman. Getting on in years. Never married. Not that she didn't have the offers. When she came out in '78, there were enough young men sniffing around. But they didn't pass muster as far as our daddy was concerned."

He punctuated the sentence with a nervous cough. "Don't

121

suppose you have any bottled water?" he asked.

"Abita Springs."

"That'll have to do."

Beautiful and gracious, I thought as I strolled to the kitchenette.

When I returned, he grabbed the glass from my hand, gulped it down and belched.

"I've got a gallon jug out there," I said. "I could roll it in."

"Stanley Fontenot didn't tell me you were such a smart ass," he said, putting the glass on the edge of my desk.

"Being of the legal profession, Stanley's always on the clock," I said. "So he gets to the point right away. Not much time for me to try out my smart ass-isms on him. But you were edging toward the problem that brought you here."

He glared at me, evidently trying to decide whether to continue our conversation or walk out the door. My vote was for the latter. Thanks to an impressive finder's fee from the Greater Southwest Insurance Co., I could afford to coast for a while. If Belladorn departed, I could get to lunch sooner. I had a taste for an oyster po'boy and The Acme was only a few blocks away from my home-office. I could take an easy stroll through the French Quarter, maybe stop off at the little frame shop on Royal to see if my "Farewell, My Lovely," movie poster was ready and then . . .

"She's a gentle woman, Manion," Samuel Belladorn said, evidently deciding to stay. "You know the kind I mean. None too worldly wise. It was daddy's fault. He was a hard son of a bitch. Demanding. Possessive. And also over-protective. If I hadn't struck out on my own when I did . . ."

I continued to frown at him and nod and let him think I was listening attentively to his achievements, but, in truth, I was focusing on the way his neck folds wiggled while they overlapped his starched collar. I tuned in again when he stopped talking about himself and returned to the subject of the weevil whose name was Neil Rosten.

"I laid ten thousand dollars, hard cash, on the desk and the bastard turned his nose up at it."

"Well, at least he isn't a cheap crook," I said. "Assuming he is a crook and not just some guy in love with your sister."

"He told Sis I tried to bribe him. Upset her pretty bad. She's . . . fragile. That wasn't the act of a man in love. It was the act of a shrewd son of a bitch trying to turn her against me."

I suspected Belladorn had done a pretty good job of that all by himself.

"Find out everything about him," he ordered, leaning forward, popping himself free from the arms of the chair. "Every little thing. Where he comes from. His daddy. His momma. Where he's been. Hell, you people know what to do in a case like this."

"He's living here in New Orleans now?"

"Somewhere up in Carrollton. I'll get the address for you."

He rose to his feet and plucked a wallet from an inside coat pocket. It was a slim leather thing that gave up two crisp thousand-dollar bills, probably from the stack Rosten had refused. He held them out, waiting for a reaction.

When I didn't throw myself across the desk grasping for them, he added a portrait of Grover Cleveland. "I'm being generous because I expect you to guarantee results."

"How would I do that?"

"I'm sure I don't have to tell you your own business. Plant some drugs on him. Get some little gal to say he raped her. I want Neil Rosten out of my hair and I don't care how you do it."

I strolled from behind my desk to the couch where he had thrown his Panama, picked it up and dropped it over the hand holding the bills. "Goodbye, Mr. Belladorn. I won't be playing with you today. You're too rough. Give my best to Sis and the weevil."

He jammed the bills into the wallet and shoved the lumpy result back into his pocket. As he waddled to my office door, he looked almost under control if you ignored the fact that his clenched fingers were tearing his hat brim.

At the door, he turned. "You might as well close up shop, Manion. You're out of business."

"For refusing to commit a crime to untie Cupid's knot?" I asked.

"No. For trying to extort money from me. The D.A., Herman Lewis, is a personal friend. Might even have him lock you up for a while, teach you a lesson." He smiled, probably at a mental picture of me wearing Angola gray with a hangdog expression on my puss. "You haven't heard the last of Samuel Belladorn."

It was his exit line, but my chuckle stopped him dead. "You think this is funny?" he growled.

"I'm amused by irony," I told him. I took the mini-cassette recorder from my pocket, rewound a portion of the tape and played it back for him. The snippet of our conversation was enough for him to get the idea. "I guess I haven't heard the last of Samuel Belladorn," I said. "Unless you're a good boy."

He left without another word, and I assumed that would be the end of our brief association.

But, a few months later, at a little after five in the evening, I picked up the ringing phone to hear his lawyer Stanley Fontenot's dry Southern accent. "Terry, I'm in my car heading for Sam Belladorn's place in the Garden District. Can you spring loose and meet me there?"

"Why? What's up?"

"A murder."

"Dare I hope it's Belladorn?"

"Sam told me you guys didn't exactly hit it off," Stanley said. "Still, you must've made an impression on him, because he asked me to bring you in on this."

"Who's dead?" I asked, thinking that Neil Rosten was the most likely victim.

"Miriam Belladorn."

"The sister?"

"No. Georgia is the sister. Miriam is . . . was Sam's wife. Whoa . . . I'm at the place now and it's wall to wall police. You coming?"

The Belladorn manse was set back from the tree-lined street by some thirty yards of lovingly cultivated landscape. A two-story affair fronted by a quartet of columns, it looked like it had been dragged behind a team of slow horses all the way from the Natchez Trace, then spruced up with white paint before the dust had time to settle.

Police cars filled the driveway and enough uniformed cops were dancing on the lawn to lend an air of urgency to the scene. Two television trucks were double-parked. They must have just arrived because the reporters were still working on their hair and makeup. I breezed past them and threaded my way through the cops until a hand grabbed my shoulder and a voice said, "Hold it, chief. Where you think you goin'?"

He was a big policeman with a sleepy, melon face. "Mr. Belladorn and his lawyer are expecting me," I told him. "My name is Manion."

"O.K. chief. Sit tight a minute, ya heah." I watched him stroll inside the house, then observed dusk descending for about five minutes before he returned. "Folla me. But keep yo' hans in yo' pockets, huh? This'a crime scene."

He led me into a long hall past ancient oil paintings of angels and saints and the Holy Family that could have come from Cardinal Richelieu's rumpus room. Directly to our right, an open doorway led to an overdone, heavily draped living room that suggested the dead woman had spent too much time in antique shops. Several cops were idly watching an African American woman in slacks, the coroner's physician, I assumed, who was kneeling on the thick carpet examining the body of the late Miriam Belladorn. The right side of the dead woman's face was painted with blood. So was the carpet. Near her outstretched right hand, a red leather wallet lay open.

"This way, chief," my guide prompted.

We moved down the hall and into a spotless white kitchen with polished utensils hanging from a ceiling rack like modern art stalactites. From there, it was out the rear door and onto a brick patio with a coy pond and a swimming pool and enough room left over for a rolling lawn that could have supported a putting green or a tennis court, if Belladorn had been at all interested in getting rid of that paunch of his.

He and Stanley Fontenot were standing near the pool beside a rather plain brunette whose slightly bulging eyes suggested she was the great man's sister, Georgia. Happily for her, there wasn't much else by way of family resemblance. Her figure, though lanky, was acceptable. And, other than the eyes, her face seemed pleasant enough, though at the moment it was the color of mildew. Her brother was patting her hand and asking if she were feeling better.

Lawyer Fontenot, a trim, dapper man with a dignified mustache who reminded me of Clifton Webb minus the ponce, gave me a crooked smile. An uncharacteristically sheepish Belladorn thanked me for coming and introduced me to his sister, who nodded politely.

Before Stanley could provide me with his game plan, two

burly NOPD detectives in rumpled sports coats and slacks rounded the corner of the house and headed our way. The older one, whose name was Boudreaux, had unblinking, probing blue eyes that he used to advantage. He was graying around the temples, without distinction, and employed a thick brush mustache to cover a long upper lip. His partner, Darvas, was a squinting, muddy-faced man with thick lips and a five-o'clock shadow. They were talking with mouths and hands, but stopped shortly before they reached us.

Boudreaux pointed a finger at me. "You the boy fren'?"

"This is Terry Manion," Stanley told him. "He works with me."

The blue eyes studied my face. "I seen you aroun', but you not a lawyer, no?"

"Private investigator," I said.

He smiled and turned to Belladorn. "Well, suh. Puttin' your team together early, eh? You know sump'n we don't?"

Belladorn gave him a puzzled look.

"I mean, you seem to be expecting the worse, eh?"

Stanley said, "Mr. Belladorn arrived home to discover his wife had been murdered. Can't get much worse than that."

"One nevah knows, do one?" Boudreaux said.

A wave of chatter rolled our way from the front of the house. "Don't take much to draw a crowd these days," Boudreaux said.

"You have statements from Mr. and Ms. Belladorn," Stanley said. "I think they'd like to go somewhere a little less hectic, until you're finished inside."

"I'd appreciate them stickin' around for just a while longer," Boudreaux said. "I got to run a errand right now, but I'll want to talk with them again when I return. Officer Darvas can keep you company."

The detective strolled jauntily back to the house. Stanley

and I exchanged glances. The fact that Boudreaux had refused to set the Belladorns free was not a good sign.

I turned to the muddy-faced Darvas. "Think you can bring me up-to-speed on the murder?"

He eyed me suspiciously.

"Just the basics, I mean. What happened, exactly?"

Darvas' eyes went to the Belladorns, who seemed too locked in their private thoughts to be paying us much attention. "The lady bought it 'bout two hours ago," he said, keeping his hoarse voice low.

"Fast work pinning the time down," I said.

"Yeah, well, a neighbor spotted this boy at the door aroun' then," Darvas said. "Funny about these houses. Real private from the street, but easy peekin' from house to house. Anyways, neighbor saw the vic open the door and invite the boy in. He ran out a few minutes later. Neighbor didn't think nothing of it at the time." Darvas rubbed the lower part of his face, not disturbing its color. "Boy musta used a silencer, otherwise the neighbor woulda heard the shot."

I scowled. "I don't suppose this watchful neighbor saw the boy get into a car, anything like that?"

Darvas shrugged. "Well, yeah. He was drivin' a classic 'vette."

"You pick him up already?"

"That's where Boudreaux was goin'."

The observant neighbor was a redhead who was a decade too old and a few pounds too plump for the pink and white-striped tights and spangled tank top she was wearing. Linette LeBlanc was a divorcee, she let me know almost immediately. Formerly wed to Raymond LeBlanc, of the Shreveport LeBlancs, a no-good bastard who had left her for "some little bimbo with a tattoo on her heinie." But she'd gotten back at

128

him. The house was hers. Ditto the weekend place in Covington, a nice new dark green Range Rover, and thirty grand a month living expenses.

I congratulated her, turned down her offer of "the best gin fizz this side of the Sazerac Bar," and moved on to the more pressing topic of the murder next door. She took me by the hand up a carpeted stairwell to a frilly pink and white bedroom in the front corner of the house. It was filled with embroidered pillows, stuffed dolls and other accouterments of someone with too much time on her hands. That included a cocktail glass with the dregs of some clear fluid resting on a tiny table. Next to it was an overstuffed pink and white chair angled toward an open window.

She pointed to the window.

It looked down on a wall separating her property from the Belladorns'. It was a high wall, but not high enough to obscure La LeBlanc's direct line of sight to the Belladorns' front door. Even in the dusk I could make out the melon face of my uniformed guide standing just to the right of it.

"I spend my afternoons downstairs in the den," Linette LeBlanc informed me while I watched a TV van snake into a section of the drive just vacated by a prowl car. "Share them with 'Days of Our Lives,' Martha Stewart and, of course, Rosie. Around two, I come up here, do a little embroidery, have a little drinkie."

"Just one drinkie?" I asked.

"Never more than one," she said. "I'm no lush, Mr. Manion. Even my ex-husband will tell you that. Anyway, I was sitting here when I heard a car on the Belladorn driveway. A little early for Sam to be coming home, so I peeked out to see who was visiting Miriam."

"Curious?" I asked.

She grinned. "Well, there's a certain amount of coming

and going over there, if you know what I mean."

"Miriam Belladorn had men visiting her?"

"Man, singular. And he sure wasn't visiting that mousy Georgia."

"Georgia lives there?"

Her eyes narrowed. "I thought you said you were working for Sam."

"As of about," I looked at my watch, "thirty-five minutes ago. I'm not quite up to speed on the family."

"I've been their neighbor for six years and I don't know much about them either. But I do know Georgia lives there."

"Pretty indiscreet of Miriam Belladorn to engage in adultery with her sister-in-law hanging around."

"Well, that's the thing. Georgia does volunteer work at Baptist Hospital until about two o'clock. Usually, Miriam and her 'friend' get it on earlier. That's why I was curious when I heard a car."

"So you looked out of this window . . . ?" I prompted.

She went through the story of the young man ringing the doorbell and being let in by Mrs. Belladorn. It took her about fifteen minutes to tell me the same thing Darvas had in less than five. The only addition was that she'd seen the boy poking around a flowerpot just off the front walkway.

Her story sounded fine to me. She was a good witness. The young guy she'd observed was definitely in the soup.

Outside, the gawkers were clogging the sidewalk and the TV newspeople were so hungry for something to do they were starting to interview one another. As they descended, shining their lights in my face, I employed my usual method for getting past them, which is to keep grinning good-naturedly while shouting the same four-letter word over and over. So much for soundbytes.

I paused beside the stone flowerpot. It was shaped like a kettle on stubby inch high legs. In the fading light that was all I could make of it without hunkering down for a closer examination.

Darvas and a uniformed cop led a tall, rawboned man in a dark suit past me and into the house. I followed them in, arriving just in time to see the newcomer nearly fall apart at the sight of the corpse. "My God. It's Miriam," he wailed.

He started swaying. I grabbed him before he hit the deck and Darvas and I helped him to a chair.

"You gonna be okay, Mr. Rosten?" the officer asked him.

Samuel Belladorn's weevil nodded, his long hair flopping over his pale forehead. He looked less like an insect than an unappreciated poet. He was maybe ten years younger than his girlfriend. "I was driving by . . . saw the lights. W-where's Georgia?" he asked.

"In back by the pool," I said.

"I want to see her." He stood.

"You oughta take it easy," Darvas said.

Rosten ignored his advice. He tested his spindly legs and then staggered from the room, me following.

Georgia Belladorn jumped to her feet as soon as she spied him. "Neil," she cried out and ran into his enveloping long arms. Her brother was staring at the couple, his face twisted as if he were in pain.

"Stanley leave?" I asked him.

"Huh?" He glared at me. "Oh, Manion. Yeah. He had some meeting or other." He tensed suddenly. I turned to see Boudreaux and Darvas marching toward us across the lawn.

"What now?" Belladorn asked despairingly.

Darvas placed a heavy hand on his shoulder. "You better come with us," he said dully.

Belladorn stared at him. "What?"

"You're undah arrest, Mr. Belladorn," Boudreaux said. "For conspirin' to murder your wife. You have the right to remain silent. Anything you say may be used in court . . ."

It was the standard Miranda litany. Not even Alec Guinness could put any life into it and Boudreaux was no Alec Guinness. Instead of listening, I pondered the word "conspirin'." When the officer finished his spiel, I asked, "The boy claim Belladorn put him up to it?"

"Somethin' like that," Boudreaux drawled and led my client away.

"I'll get Stanley," I called after them. Belladorn just raised his shoulders in a shrug. He was a whipped dog.

Georgia tore away from her boyfriend's clutches and ran after them. They all disappeared into the house. Neil Rosten sidled up to me. "They arresting him?" he asked, as if the idea appealed to him.

"Sure looks that way," I said.

The front of the house suddenly lit up like the aurora borealis. The TV news folks were getting the footage they'd come for. I went inside to phone Stanley Fontenot and tell him about all the fun he'd missed.

The next morning Stanley and I visited our client in a cell in the City Jail section of the Criminal Courts Building on Tulane Avenue. Belladorn sat with his hands in his lap. He looked listless and unfocused. The odor of pine oil disinfectant was so strong it made my eyes water.

"Sorry you had to spend the night here," Stanley said. "I've got Judge Clement working on bail. The boy said you hired him to kill Miriam."

"It's a lie. I loved her, Stanley. You know that."

The lawyer nodded. "Herman Lewis feels he has enough

to indict you," he said.

"Isn't that the same D.A. you said was such a good friend of yours?" I asked Belladorn.

His woeful eyes shifted to me. "You come here to gloat, Manion?"

It *had* been a cheap shot.

Stanley gave me a look of disapproval that changed into a grin of confidence when he addressed the client. "Actually, Terry's got a few ideas that may help."

Belladorn turned toward me again. It seemed an effort for him to move his head. "Like what?" he asked.

"I don't want to raise any false hopes," I said. "But there are a few things worth exploring."

"If it's money you need . . ."

I sighed. "What I need is to know how far you want me to go?"

"I don't understand."

"Stanley will be happy with you back on the street a free man," I said. "You want me to stop there or do you want me to find the person who really hired the kid?"

He didn't answer at first. Then he said softly, "I want Miriam's murderer brought to justice. Why wouldn't I want that?"

"I can almost guarantee it won't be a stranger."

He blinked. "I want her killer punished," he said without equivocation.

"You're the boss," I said.

My next stop was Robbery-Homicide. Boudreaux greeted me with a cold, blue-eyed stare and a mustache twitch. Darvas, on the phone, shifted in his chair and turned away from me.

"Can I talk to the hit boy?" I asked Boudreaux.

"That's easy to answer, shamus. No."

"Then maybe you could help me out?"

"Be surprised if that's so."

"The boy make a definite ID of Belladorn?"

"The hit was set up by phone. The boy, Del MacDermott, never actually eyeballed him, if that's your angle."

"But he can identify the voice?"

"None of your damn business," Boudreaux snapped, so loudly Darvas hung up his phone to gawk at us. The older cop calmed down and added, "Voice was muffled, but the callah identified himself as Belladorn."

"Lucky for you he didn't say he was the mayor," I said.

"Get outa heah, Manion. They shouldn't 'a let you in heah in the first place."

"The boy actually name Miriam Belladorn as his intended victim?" I asked, ignoring his request.

"What kinda question . . . oh, I see what you're sayin'." He thought about it. "I don't believe so. Darvas?"

The muddy-faced detective consulted a sheaf of typewritten pages on his desk. He paused at one, read it carefully and said, "His instructions were to go to the house, ring the bell and hit the woman who answered the door and accepted the message."

"Ordinarily, there were three women in that house," I said. "Belladorn's wife, his sister and the maid."

"Maid's only there in the morning," Boudreaux said. "Long gone by eleven."

"What about the sister?"

"At the dentist's," Darvas said. "I checked."

"So the person who hired the killer knew the maid would be gone and Georgia would be getting her teeth drilled," I said.

"Belladorn would know that, yeah," Boudreaux said. "Now, if that's all . . ."

134

My mind was racing over the facts as I knew them. "MacDermott said he was told to shoot the woman who accepted the message?"

"That's what he said."

"Could I see the message?"

Boudreaux frowned and turned to Darvas who seemed puzzled. "Damned if it was in the inventory," he said. "Maybe the kid took it with him."

"No," Boudreaux grumbled. "Check his statement."

Darvas shuffled pages and read, " '. . . the bitch comes to the door and I hand her the message and she takes it inside to get me a tip. I step inside, too, whip out the Eagle-5, all silenced up. Pop-pop and I'm outa there.' "

"Nothing about him stopping to take the message back."

"We better ask him," Boudreaux said.

"While you're at it, you might want to find out where it came from, since he had no physical contact with his employer. And how exactly was he expecting to get paid?"

Boudreaux grabbed the phone and arranged to have the kid brought to one of the interrogation rooms. Then he ordered Darvas to beat it to the Belladorn home to see if the message had turned up there.

"C'mon," Boudreaux told me. "You earned a seat."

I followed him to a small windowless but well-lighted room furnished by three metal chairs and a metal table. The room was painted in shades of brown and smelled of stale vinegar. Boudreaux pulled up a chair. I leaned against a wall.

Del MacDermott was a stringy kid just past the juvie stage, with the shaggy start of a beard peeking through the acne. He was loud and brash. He was too young to care about the penalty for murder. He was too young to care about much of anything.

"You gonna ask me more questions? Where's my shy-lock?"

"Gee, Del," Boudreaux said, "you already confessed to killin' the woman. You really want your lawyer, we'll get 'im."

Del waved a magnanimous hand. "Forget 'im."

"You told us you never actually saw Samuel Belladorn, right?"

"Naw. He phones me and says me it's worth twenty large to make the kill. I say it sounds good to me."

"Where'd you get the message you was supposed to delivah?"

"Same place I got the dough. In a brown envelope under a flowerpot in front of the place."

That checked with what Linette LeBlanc had told me.

"Belladorn must be a real jagoff," Boudreaux said, "trustin' you to do the job after you got your mitts on the money."

Del MacDermott stuck out his chin. "Hey, I'm a professional. I don't take money 'less I earn it."

"Excuse me all to hell for suggestin' otherwise," Boudreaux said.

"Whose name was on the message?" I asked.

The kid looked at me, then at Boudreaux in exasperation. "The lady who answered the door. Who else?"

"Miriam Belladorn?" I asked.

"Yeah."

"Sure the message wasn't for Georgia Belladorn?"

Boudreaux leaned forward in his chair.

"It was for the one I popped," the boy said defensively.

"Which one was that?" I asked.

"The one that took the goddamned message."

Boudreaux rubbed his eyes with a knuckle. He rose, went

to the door and opened it. "Take Mistah MacDermott back to his suite," he told the cop waiting there.

"You going to phone the Belladorn house?" I asked as we walked back to his desk. "Darvas should be there by now."

He was, and he'd located the message. After a few heated questions, Boudreaux slammed down the phone in a gesture of frustration. "The message was addressed to Georgia Belladorn," he said. "The kid screwed the pooch. Killed the wrong woman. Some professional.

"Not that this cuts your client any slack. Now we got a better motive than jealousy. Jealousy will do, but murder for profit, that's gold. Sometimes a jury'll let a crime of passion slide. But a premeditated killing for money, that's about as good as it gets for the prosecution."

"What money are we talking about?" I asked.

"Belladorn and his sister split like twenty mil when their old man passed away. Georgia Belladorn having no other known relations or descendants, her estate goes to big brother. Geeze, shamus, you ever think of checking on your client's background?"

I thanked him for the suggestion and for his cooperation and got out of there.

Darvas was just leaving the columned home when I arrived. I asked him if Georgia Belladorn was inside.

"Rosten's with her. She's actin' kinda weird."

"Weird like how?"

"Jumpy, nervous. Cryin'."

"You tell her she was the intended victim?"

He nodded. "She heard me on the phone. She said the vic was the one supposed to get her teeth cleaned. Except she thought she was catching a cold, so Georgia Belladorn took her appointment."

"And Miriam took Georgia's," I said.

I turned to look at the LeBlanc home. There was no light in the upstairs window. I wondered if Linette was up there, watching.

"Are they alone in there?" I asked Darvas.

"I left a uniform. Something up?"

"Stick around and see," I told him.

The policeman on duty was seated in a chair in the hall, beside the door to a room that I supposed was a study—dark wood cabinets filled with books, a bar, TV set, soft rugs on the floor, brown leather men's club chairs. The couple was perched on a matching leather couch, Rosten near the middle, Georgia all the way to one end. I'd heard his voice as we approached, but he went silent when we entered.

"Sorry to bother you, Ms. Belladorn," I said, "but would you join Officer Darvas and me for a minute?"

She started to rise, but Rosten grabbed her arm. "What do you want with her?" he asked me sharply.

The edge in Rosten's voice caused Darvas to stiffen. The duty cop wandered in.

Georgia Belladorn pulled from the young man's grasp and walked toward us. "What is it you want, Mr. Manion?" she asked very calmly.

"I wanted you away from him," I said. "He might have tried something foolish before Darvas could arrest him for your sister-in-law's murder."

Darvas' mouth snapped shut like a nutcracker. "I don't suppose this comes as a surprise to you, ma'am," I said to Georgia Belladorn, "since you already know you were the intended victim."

"Why would Neil want me dead?" she asked, as if it were the only thing she hadn't figured out.

The two cops were now flanking Rosten.

"He and your sister-in-law were . . . involved," I said. "Ms. LeBlanc, from next door, saw him come to the house often when you weren't here." I neglected to mention that I hadn't realized until five minutes ago the implication of Ms. LeBlanc's comment that the man calling on Miriam Belladorn ". . . sure wasn't visiting that mousy Georgia."

Rosten's eyes narrowed. "My God, darling, you can't believe any of this?"

"You blew it," I told him. "The only reason someone would work out such an elaborate scheme with a hired gun would be to keep his identity a secret. But you had to go ahead and say you were Samuel Belladorn. He may be impetuous and arrogant and quite impressed by his own name, but he isn't stupid."

"This is crap," Rosten said. "I love Georgia. Why would I want her dead?"

"She dies, her money goes to her brother. He's convicted of murdering her and the fortune bounces to his wife, whom you marry when she's free. Were you thinking of getting rid of her somewhere down the road?"

"Don't listen to this insanity, Georgia."

But she was listening, her slightly protruding eyes studying him like a bug on a pin.

"You nearly passed out when you discovered the wrong Belladorn woman had been killed," I said. "But then you realized Miriam and Georgia were interchangeable. The surviving one gets the dough . . . and, consequently, you."

"He's in league with your brother, Georgia," Rosten shouted. "They're trying to set him free and get rid of me."

I realized, looking at him, that if I'd taken Belladorn's original offer, I'd have found out about Miriam and Rosten, she'd be alive and I'd be three grand richer. It made me even more annoyed with him.

"The clincher is the twenty thousand it took to do the job," I said. "You and I, Neil, we don't have that kind of money at our fingertips. My guess is you borrowed it from somebody very close to you. Somebody like . . . well, like Ms. Belladorn here. Possibly you told her it was for an important investment of some kind. The police would never think of looking into the murdered woman's bank account for a withdrawal of the money paid to have her killed.

"Thing is, she isn't dead. So we can ask her about it."

Georgia Belladorn nodded with a touch of regret. "Over the past several months I've given him at least that much. For business, he told me. To secure our future."

Rosten leapt up from the couch, startling Darvas, who grabbed his shoulder. "What are you saying, Georgia? You didn't give me any money."

Darvas smiled and got a firmer grip on him. "Everybody's lyin' but you, huh?" he said. "Well, you can tell us all about it after we get you booked."

When the front door had shut on Darvas and Rosten, I turned to Georgia Belladorn. "I'm sorry about all this. You're a very strong woman."

She shook her head. "No, I'm my brother's little sister. I make foolish mistakes and he's always right. Always. But this time I thought . . ."

She didn't finish the sentence, but I knew what she thought. Or I assumed I did.

It only goes to show.

That night I was awakened from a sound sleep by a phone call from Boudreaux. He said, "Hey, podnah, you do nice work."

"What the hell time is it?" I asked, trying to get my bearings in the dark bedroom.

"It's two-twenty-eight in the ayem. An' he's dead as the dormouse." He laughed.

"Who's dead?" I asked, shaking the sleep from my head.

"Your client."

I sat up.

"An hour after we drive him home," Boudreaux continued, "his sister emptied a gun into him. Messy, tres messy."

A sharp pain was piercing my skull.

"I was wonderin' if you got any idea why she did it, shamus," Boudreaux said. "She's not talkin'. Not doin' much of anythin' ac'shully. Mind went bye-bye on her."

"She said something about her brother always being right," I told him. "I guess he rubbed her nose in it one time too many."

"The thing is," Boudreaux said, "the D.A. don't think we can make the Miriam Belladorn killing stick to Rosten now. Even if Georgia was to come back down to earth, all we'd have is the word of a homicidal loony-tune that she fronted him the money to pay the shooter. And that wouldn't float in court, not even in these screwball times."

"Well, at least he won't profit from his crime."

"I'm not so sure 'bout that," the detective chuckled. "Rosten claims you and the Belladorns conspired to railroad him and he's planning on suing you and the estate. So sleep well, shamus. Your client's murdered, his sister's headed for the funny farm and you gonna be up to your ass in lawyers."

Another case marked "solved" by Terry Manion, ace detective, I thought as I hung up the phone. I plowed my head deep into the feather pillow, but it was a useless gesture. I wouldn't be getting back to sleep for a while.

Murder at Mardi Gras

J.J. Legendre's watch read 9:24 as he reached out for the ringing phone. Nine-twenty-four, on an oddly warm Monday night in February in the city of New Orleans, 1967. A few blocks away, the Crew of Proteus, fourth oldest Mardi Gras parading organization, was rolling its huge, gaudy floats down Rampart Street. J.J. could hear the rattle of the drums and the yelling of the crowd over the sound of the 12" black and white Philco he'd been watching.

"Legendre," he announced laconically to his caller.

"Me, Lee-john," district attorney Jim Garrison's booming voice informed him. "Surprised you're not out among 'em, watchin' the parade."

"Seen all the Mardi Gras I care to," J.J. said. "I don't like crowds, specially when they're full of amateur drinkers."

"Afraid you're gonna have to put up with 'em tonight," Garrison said. "Get on over to the Lacombe house on St. Charles."

J.J. didn't have to ask the exact address of the three-story mansion where the family of the late ex-governor of Louisiana, Edmund Lacombe, resided. He'd lived in the city for nine years and served as a homicide detective on the New Orleans Police Department for most of that time before becoming an investigator for Garrison's office. "Who's dead?" he asked.

"The daughter-in-law, Kim Lacombe. Now get rolling. The way those NOPD space cadets screw around, the corpse could wind up heading down Canal Street on a float."

J.J. replaced the receiver, cast a wistful look at Marshall Matt Dillon lumbering across the flickering TV screen. He continued to watch the show as he put on his shirt and tie, slipped into his shoes.

In the bedroom, he strapped on his weapon rig and got into his suit coat. He surveyed his image in the mirror over his dresser. Betraying a streak of vanity, he ran a brush over his hair and used his thumb and finger to smooth down his thin moustache.

He decided not to turn off the TV set. It was a lousy substitute for human companionship, but it was better than coming home to an apartment that was empty and silent. Before heading out, he waited for Marshal Matt to gun down the young hotshot who'd been terrorizing Dodge City. "The lawman always wins," he said to the room. "On the tube."

There were still stragglers scuffling along the avenue in front of the Lacombe mansion, searching the ground for trinkets and coins tossed by the parade's masked revelers. J.J., who'd had to park three blocks away, rushed past them and through the wrought iron gate leading to the columned building.

He recognized the homicide detectives, Lieutenant Daniel Abadie and Officer Sonny Voire. He'd worked with them on the NOPD and had worked around them thereafter. Abadie was an officious, wiry little guy with a small scar extending upward from the corner of his mouth. It looked like a dueling scar, but J.J. doubted that the man knew the difference between an epee and an etouffe. The sturdy, bull-necked Voire wasn't a bad sort, merely dim. Garrison had been wise to put J.J. on the case.

Neither policeman was happy to see him.

"Whatcha doin' here, Cajun?" Voire asked. "We got this wrapped up."

J.J., who was not a Cajun but had learned to live with the nickname, said, "Mind unwrapping it to give me a little peek, Sonny?"

Voire looked at his superior, who rewarded J.J. with a shark's grin. "Sure 'nuf, Lejern," Abadie said. "Then you can go back, tell the big man we got ever'thin' unner control. He can concentrate his effuts worryin' about the JFK hit squad an' leave the local murders to us."

The two policemen led the way to an upstairs bedroom where Dr. Joseph Macaluso from the coroner's office was supervising the removal of the body of a young Asian woman. J.J. gave the room a quick survey, noting the excessive amount of blood.

Abadie pointed to scissors, coated in red, resting on the beige carpet. "They did the job, looks like." He turned to Dr. Macaluso. "Got any news fo' us, doc?"

"Victim died hard: she was severely beaten before she was stabbed," the doctor replied. He was a big, soft-looking man wearing his usual black suit, starched white shirt, black tie and sour expression of disapproval. His brother was a priest at St. Stevens and J.J. thought that Macaluso might have been happier in that calling, too.

"Anything else?" he asked.

Macaluso's scowl deepened and he pursed his lips. "The victim appears to have been . . . no, I'd rather not speculate."

"Come on, doc," Abadie urged.

"You'll have to wait until after I've had her on the table," Dr. Macaluso said firmly before making his exit.

"Thanks for all yo' he'p, doc," Abadie called after him sar-

145

castically. He turned to the others. "Well, hell, at least we know who done it."

"Oh?" J.J. asked.

"The goddamn Mardi Gras Burglar," Voire said, "an' he's sure bought himself some serious trouble this time." His reference was to an enterprising sneak thief who'd been taking advantage of the fact that many wealthy and prominent families fled the city at Mardi Gras to escape the noise, the crowds, the traffic and, in some cases, the anti-Semitism of the carnival organizations.

"I thought he only hit homes that were unoccupied," J.J. said.

Voire waved a dismissive hand. "He probably thought the place *was* empty. The Lacombes was havin' a few frens ovah to watch the parade. They was all out lookin' at the floats."

"Nobody home? Not even servants?"

"Well, yeah, servants," Voire said. "Cook and maid, downstairs in the kitchen."

"Like Sonny sez," Abadie added, "Ever'body was outside. The victim wasn't feelin' up to it, so she came back in. Once the floats passed, the others came in, too. Her husband," he pointed to a framed photograph on the dressing table, "he strolled up here to see how she was doin'. Found her, dead as a doorknob."

"This the gov's son, huh?" J.J. asked. The color photo was of a handsome young man in an Army officer's uniform proudly accepting a medal from President Lyndon Johnson.

Abadie nodded. "Yep. Edmund Arthur Lacombe, Jr. And that there, Lejern, is the Purple Heart."

"How's he handling his wife's death?" J.J. asked, replacing the photograph.

"No so hot," Abadie said.

"Times like this, it don't matter who your ole man was or

how brave you were," Voire said in a surprising display of empathy. "You gotta do some grievin'."

"Anybody happened to see or hear the thief?" J.J. asked.

Abadie shook his head. "Nope. Less'n you count the dead woman. She seen him real up close, I imagine."

"The folks were all out front so he had to of gone out the way he come in," Voire offered, pointing to French doors leading to a rear balcony. A panel near the door handle had been shattered.

J.J. walked to the door, careful to avoid the glass shards glittering like diamonds on the carpet. He used a pen to raise one of the door handles and open the door.

Without leaving the bedroom, he hunkered down to concentrate on the lighted balcony platform, then looked at the door lock.

He was conscious of the two policemen staring at him as he rose and turned back to the room. Ignoring them, he made a tour of the bedroom, pausing to consider a few items—slippers under the bed, a large ashtray on a bedside table, a woman's watch on another small table, beside a telephone, a walking stick with a heavy knob resting upright in a corner of the room.

"You guys didn't disturb anything in here?" he asked.

"We look like amachoors?" Abadie asked.

J.J. bit his tongue. "Anything missing, you know of?"

Abadie pointed to a chifforobe. The second of its six drawers hung open. "Victim musta surprised the guy goin' through her stuff. Looks like he didn't get much further than that drawer."

J.J. looked into the drawer. It contained bits of clothing material, buttons, a pin cushion, another pair of scissors. He scanned the room again, noting the place where the dead woman fell, the position of the murder weapon. "Where's that go?" he asked, pointing to a closed door.

"Closet," Abadie said, using his elbow to push the door open on a huge walk-in closet. On one side was an array of women's clothes hanging somewhat haphazardly. On the other was a row of men's suits and sport coats neatly arranged. Above them was a shelf containing folded dress shirts, most of them white. On the floor was a row of polished men's shoes all in trees.

"Neat sort of fella," J.J. observed. "Except for this." He pointed to a small object that rested directly beneath two empty coat hangers.

Abadie moved closer, squinting. "It's a Mardi Gras coin. From the parade. Bag it, Voire. Might have the Burglar's prints on it."

J.J. asked Abadie, "You've kept everybody here, right?"

"I was about to send 'em on their way," Abadie said.

"Not just yet," J.J. said.

"They're squawkin'," Voire whined. "Most of 'em are on a first-name basis with the mayor. And it's not like they're suspects."

"No?" J.J. asked.

"We know who did this, Lejern," Abadie said. "The Mardi Gras Burglar. All we got to do is catch him. And we will."

"There's no broken glass on the balcony," J.J. said.

"Of course not," Abadie said. "He was standin' out there when he smashed the window in. Glass is on the inside, on the rug."

"But if he went out the way he came in—and, as Sonny correctly noted, that's what he would have done—he'd have tracked at least a couple shards back out there with him. I bet you won't find any scuff marks on the railing, either. But there are some fresh scratches on that walking stick knob that look like they could have been caused by jagged glass."

Abadie looked flustered. "You sayin' what, then?"

"I'm saying we should go talk to the folks downstairs."

Nine people were gathered in the living room. J.J. introduced himself to them, trying not to be too influenced by his first impressions. The dignified fifty-something Dr. Jarman Bodet seemed properly somber, but his wife, Claire, a handsome brunette at least two decades younger, sipped her cocktail as if she were still enjoying the party. She seemed overly attentive to the group's only bachelor, Paul Crain, an almost too handsome Army buddy of Edmund Lacombe's whose mind seemed a hundred miles away. His date, a sarcastic young socialite named Glory Perrin, was anxious to leave, possibly because she feared Crain would start responding to Claire Bodet's signals.

The elegant, preening Bertrands, Glenn and Carlotta, sipped their martinis at a far corner of the room, as if they were hoping to distance themselves from the unpleasantness. The maid, a thirtyish black woman in livery named Cecelia Davis, seemed to be doing the same thing at the opposite corner.

J.J. filed his mental snapshots and focused on the new widower. Edmund Lacombe, Jr. sat slumped on a sofa, glassy-eyed, his brown tweed sports coat twisted under his thin body. The right leg of his dark blue trousers had risen high enough to display eight inches of blue sock secured by a foulard garter. He was being consoled by a tall, imposing woman with gray hair—his mother, Alice, the late governor's wife.

She withdrew her arm from around her son's shoulders and addressed J.J., "Tell me one thing, sir: why in heaven's name can't you people leave us alone in our grief?"

"Just doing our job, Mrs. Lacombe."

"Your job? Your job is to find the monster who entered my home and murdered my daughter-in-law and my grand-child."

"Your gran'chile?" Abadie asked, surprise cracking his voice and making him sound almost adolescent.

J.J. recalled Dr. Macaluso's unspoken suspicion. "Your wife was pregnant?" he asked Edmund Lacombe.

The distraught young man turned toward him. He opened his mouth and croaked, "She was . . ."

"Kim was carrying my grandchild," Mrs. Lacombe said. "As I discovered tonight, thanks to Dr. Bodet."

The middle-aged man in a dark gray suit frowned and said to J.J., "Kim was my patient. I confirmed her pregnancy several weeks ago." He faced Mrs. Lacombe. "I assumed you knew."

The elderly woman sighed and said, somewhat bitterly, "Kim was from a culture that prizes secrecy."

"We weren't trying to keep it a secret, mother," her son said defensively, straightening on the couch. "We didn't want you to get your hopes up until we were sure . . . So many things can go wrong this early."

The thing that did go wrong brought tears to his eyes.

Alice Lacombe gave her son a brave smile, then wheeled on J.J. "We've tolerated your presence long enough, I think," she said.

"I'm sorry, Mrs. Lacombe," he said, "But I'm going to have to impose upon you and your guests a little longer. I've got a few questions to ask."

"Why, in God's name?"

"To help us get a picture of how your daughter-in-law was killed," J.J. said innocently.

Alice Lacombe seethed in silence for several seconds, then said, "Do it quickly."

"Is there a room I can use?"

It was decided that the interviews be conducted in the late governor's den, a comfortable room with shelves of books and a huge family oil portrait over a fireplace so spotless, J.J. wondered if it was ever used.

A heavy desk, glistening with furniture polish, faced out from a wall of mullioned windows. J.J. ignored it in favor of a more informal setting—a soft leather sofa and armchair grouping in front of the fireplace. To his amusement, Lt. Abadie opted for the power position at the desk, while Voire, notepad in fist, sat just to the right of his boss.

"Don't mind us, Lejern," Abadie told him with a grin. "We'll just sit here and see how it's done."

J.J. hoped that was the truth. It was his belief that the closer he could get to simulating a one-on-one atmosphere, the more successful the interview would be.

"You've got men keeping an eye on the folks out there, right? And somebody upstairs to watch over the crime scene?" J.J. asked.

"This ain't our first homicide, Lejern."

"Okay, let's get this done," J.J. said.

He deposed the maid quickly. She knew nothing about the crime, had heard nothing. She confirmed that the cook had left the premises (and two machine loads of dirty dishes) just before the parade passed; in other words, before Kim Lacombe had returned to her room to meet her death.

J.J. thought he could gauge her feelings about the deceased by her absence of emotion, but he asked anyway. "Miz Kim was okay," Cecelia told him. "Maybe a little demanding. But I'm used to that."

"You didn't hear her return from the parade?"

"No, suh. The dishwasher makes some racket. Can't hear yourself think."

She hadn't heard the glass windowpane break either.

★ ★ ★ ★ ★

"You're the office manager of Lacombe Industries?" J.J. asked the blasé Glenn Bertrand.

"That's my title, yes."

J.J. couldn't quite place the accent. Eastern seaboard. Affected British. He didn't like it or the man's smug smile. "So you work for Edmund Lacombe?" he asked.

"Eddie is a . . . spokesman for the company," Bertrand said. "He's genial. He dresses well. Belongs to the right clubs. But he's not terribly involved in the day-to-day operation. I run the company for him. And for Alice, of course."

"It's a privately-owned company?"

"Yes."

"With Edmund Lacombe and his mother holding equal shares?"

Bertrand stared at J.J. "I don't see what bearing that could have on your investigation, detective."

"One never knows. But if it makes you uncomfortable, we'll move on. Tell me everything you did after the parade."

"Kim returned early. The rest of us drifted back at our own speeds. Carlotta and I went to the living room. I went to the temporary bar and poured us both martinis."

"Were you alone?"

"Briefly. Then Paul and Glory joined us, the doctor and his wife and Alice and Edmund."

"You and Mrs. Bertrand were together from the time of the parade until Edmund discovered his wife's body?"

"We were."

"How well did you know Kim Lacombe?"

"Not well. We've had a few dinners together. She and Eddie moved in a different social circle than my wife and I."

"Tell me about their social circle."

"The Boston Club. The Country Club. New Orleans society. Carlotta and I prefer a slightly more sophisticated milieu."

"Society?" Abadie squawked. "Man was married to a yeller. Not many o' them in society."

Bertrand twisted his neck to regard the lieutenant. "In the New Orleans society game, patriotism trumps race," he said. "Wounded war hero falls in love with little native nursey who helped him walk again. They were the toast of the town.

"Anyway, even those diehard old Southern bigots had no choice but to accept Kim. Alice isn't someone you want to anger. You gentlemen might take that to heart yourselves. Now, if that's all . . ."

"How did *Alice* feel about Kim?" J.J. asked, ignoring the man's impatience.

"You'll have to ask her, if you're brave enough."

Bertrand's wife, Carlotta, didn't mind answering the question. Sitting on the sofa in the precise spot vacated by her husband, she said in between puffs on a black cigarette with a shiny, gold-colored filter, "Alice was fit to be tied. At least when Eddie phoned her from Vietnam with the news."

"And later?"

"When she calmed down, I believe she accepted the inevitable."

"What did *you* think of Kim?" J.J. asked.

Carlotta Bertrand flipped cigarette ash onto the carpet. "I thought she was a devious, self-serving little bitch."

"Don't hold back now," J.J. said.

She smiled. "All right. Here's my version of the Eddie and Little Kim Story. He's a mama's boy-idiot who pays more attention to his wardrobe than he does to his company. Kim had enough ambition for them both and she . . . took advantage of her situation."

"How's that?"

"A few weeks ago, at another of these dreadful dinners Alice hinted that she was considering a vice-presidency for Glenn at Lacombe. Kim nearly choked on her Shrimp Remoulade. I could tell what was going on in that aggressive little mind. A promotion for Glenn was a clear sign as to who was really running the company. As soon as we were out the door, Kim was bending mother-in-law's ear with reasons why Glenn's vice-presidency would be a mistake."

"You know that for a fact?"

"What I know," Carlotta Bertand said, "is that Alice called Glenn aside earlier tonight and told him she'd reconsidered and thought a raise might be more appropriate. A *raise*."

"Maybe Mrs. Lacombe simply changed her mind on her own."

"You wouldn't think so, if you'd seen sweet little Kim grinning at us all through dinner. Do you know what bile tastes like, Detective Legendre?"

"I've sampled it once or twice," J.J. said. "Could you tell me what you did after the parade?"

"Everything? My, my. Including my trip to the little girl's room?"

"I don't need the specifics," J.J. said with a smile. "Just the general time frame."

"Well, Glenn and I returned to the house, to the living room which was empty. He fixed drinks while I went to the powder room. I returned just as Paul and his little ill-tempered debutante wandered in. She must be the greatest lay in the world for Paul to put up with her. Maybe she took lessons from little Kim. Can I please go now?"

When J.J. had escorted her out the door, Voire said,

"Geeze, there's a bitch and a half. I could see her usin' them scissors."

" 'cept she didn't," Abadie said.

"What makes you think so?" J.J. asked.

"There was a lot of blood upstairs," Abadie said. "You see any blood on her, Lejern?"

"Just in her eye," J.J. replied.

"None of 'em got any blood on 'em," Abadie said scornfully. "The guy with the victim's blood on him, the Burglar, got away off the balcony. This is a waste of time."

"Don't let me keep you, lieutenant," J.J. said.

Abadie sighed. "Bring 'em on," he said wearily.

Dr. Jarman Bodet sat stiffly on the couch and announced that he really didn't feel he had anything to contribute to the investigation.

"How long have you been the Lacombe family physician?" J.J. asked.

"I'm not a general practitioner," Dr. Bodet replied with a hint of indignation. "My wife and I have been friends of the Lacombes for a long time. Edmund, Senior, and I were in Kappa Alpha together at Tulane."

"But you treated Kim Lacombe," J.J. said.

"Yes. I'm a gynecologist. Mrs. Lacombe is my patient also."

"What was your impression of Kim Lacombe, doctor?"

"I can give you my *personal* impression. She was quiet, attentive, bright."

"And pregnant."

"As you heard."

"Anything unusual about the pregnancy?"

"No. Everything seemed normal."

"Can you think of any reason why she would have kept the

pregnancy a secret from Mrs. Lacombe?"

"No. Other than what Edmund offered."

"Once the parade ended, did you and Mrs. Bodet return to the house immediately?"

"We strolled back. I believe we walked in just ahead of Alice and Edmund."

"Where was everyone when you entered?"

"Hmmm. Edmund and Alice were right behind us. Paul and the Perrin girl were talking near the piano. Glenn was fixing a drink at the bar. I headed for the rest room and passed Carlotta on my way."

"Was there a lot of talk about Kim Lacombe's pregnancy?"

"Oh, yes. I felt like an idiot, mentioning it at dinner. But she hadn't said anything about keeping it a secret from Alice."

"What was Alice Lacombe's reaction?"

The doctor hesitated. "She was a bit upset. More with Eddie than Kim, by my measure."

"By the way, do you happen to know who *is* the Lacombe family doctor?"

"Charles Didier is their internist," Dr. Bodet replied, a puzzled frown creasing his forehead.

"Thank you, doctor."

Nina Bodet was the doctor's second wife, she informed them. "The original lives in Metairie with their two boys and a dog. We see the boys on weekends. The ex-wife and the dog, we rarely if ever see. Does that about cover it?"

"It's all very interesting, ma'am," J.J. said, "but maybe you could tell us a little about what went on right after the parade passed."

"Jarman and I walked back to the house with Alice and

Edmund. Kim had already returned. I went to the kitchen to see if the cook could squeeze another cup of coffee from the pot, but the kitchen was empty and so was the pot."

"Nobody was in the kitchen?"

"Not a soul."

"What can you tell me about Kim Lacombe?" J.J. asked.

Claire Bodet's attractive face hardened for a brief moment, then relaxed into a smile. "What would you like to know about Kim?"

"Did she get along with people?"

"Why would you ask such a thing?"

"I gather some folks didn't care much for her."

"You mean Glory?"

"Glory Perrin?" J.J. asked. "They weren't friends?"

"Glory was affianced to Edmund before he went to Vietnam. No. Not friends at all."

"How did you get along with Kim Lacombe, Mrs. Bodet?"

"You're a very handsome man, detective," she said. "I like a man with a moustache."

J.J. thanked her for the compliment and repeated the question. She hesitated, then asked, "Why aren't you in Vietnam?"

"Luck of the draw, I guess."

"Well, my baby brother wasn't so lucky. He was killed by a sniper somewhere in the Mekong delta. So I guess you'd say my feelings toward Kim were . . . ambivalent."

"Because she was Vietnamese?"

"My family calls them gooks," Claire Bodet said sweetly. "That answer your question?"

Unlike the others, Paul Crain seemed deeply and sincerely saddened by the murder. "She was a good woman," he said, his eyes moist. "A healer. A nurturer."

"You were in the Army with Edmund?" J.J. asked.

"Actually, I met them both at around the same time. I spent three months in a hospital bed next to Eddie's, recovering from a million dollar bullet wound and a shattered collarbone. Kim nursed us both back to health."

"How'd you feel about her marrying Edmund?"

"Great. They're both great people. She . . . *was* a great person."

"You don't sound like you're from New Orleans?"

"Detroit City," Crain said. "Was there working for GM when Edmund called and told me he and Kim had tied the knot and were whooping it up down here. Offered me a job with Lacombe. I didn't come at first. But then, there were cutbacks at GM and . . . here I am."

"You and Ms. Perrin a couple?"

"Glory and I? We kick around together," Paul Crain said.

Glory Perrin was bored and anxious to leave. In the midst of questions regarding her activities just before the discovery of Kim Lacombe's body, she informed J.J. that her father was the Perrin in the law firm of Clay, Perrin and Whitley. They represented not only the Lacombe family but just about every other socially prominent family in the city.

"And, you know, I'm feeling downright litigious at the moment," she said.

"Then we'll move right along," J.J. told her. "Did Edmund Lacombe's marriage take you by surprise?"

She stared at him. "It took everyone by surprise," she said.

"But not everybody had been engaged to him."

"What exactly is your point, Detective?"

"My point is to find out as much as I can about Kim Lacombe and the people who knew her. You knew her. I would imagine you might have resented a woman who married your fiancé."

"I suppose I resented her. But when I really thought about it, I decided she saved me from a serious mistake. Edmund is not exactly a wonder boy. His mother won't live forever, and then, who'll take care of things?"

"Was the idea that Kim would?"

"You'll have to ask Alice that," Glory Perrin said. "Frankly, I would have thought so, until tonight at the parade. You should have seen her running around chasing those cheap Mardi Gras trinkets like a dim-witted two-dollar tramp. Oh, my, did I just say that. Daddy would be furious at me for speaking ill of the dead."

J.J. had an assortment of questions for Edmund Lacombe, but realized almost immediately that he was not going to get the chance to voice them. The young man was in what appeared to be a mild state of shock. His concentration was shot. Tears filled his eyes at the mere mention of his late wife's name.

"I . . . I'm sorry, sir," he said to J.J., "I just can't do . . . this."

His mother was scarcely more forthcoming. "I think this is idiotic and you, sir, are an unnecessary nuisance. I'll be sure to pass my opinion on to your supervisor."

"That would be District Attorney Garrison," J.J. said.

"Of course it would. That fool."

Well, the D.A. *was* a figure of controversy. "Do you like Glory Perrin, ma'am?" J.J. asked.

"What an odd question. Why would you ask such a thing?"

"She almost became your daughter-in-law. Were you disappointed that she didn't?"

"I've known the Perrins for years. It would have been a

good match. But Edmund and Kim fell in love, and that was that."

"Is that a spot on your sleeve?" J.J. asked.

Alice Lacombe looked down at a dark red stain the size of a quarter near the cuff of her right sleeve. "These wild children nearly knocked me down while I was watching the parade. One of them was drinking some red soda."

"Mr. Bertrand wouldn't answer any of my questions about Lacombe Industries," J.J. said.

"Mr. Bertrand is no fool."

"It is a family-owned business, right?"

"Yes."

"With you and your son equal share holders?"

"It's a bit more complicated than that."

"Was there anything in the late governor's will about grandchildren?"

She stood, red spots of anger appearing on her cheeks. "That's enough now," she said, controlling her rage. "I've indulged you. Now you must leave."

"I'm sorry," J.J. said, "but I have one more favor, ma'am. I really have to use that phone. It'll be a local call."

"Yes, yes, anything. Just be done with it, for God's sake."

She strode from the room.

"That's one pissed-off lady, Cajun," Voire said.

"Yeah, Lejern, you dived into the soup and dragged us in with you."

J.J. wasn't paying them much attention. He was dialing the D.A.'s special number. Garrison answered on the third ring. "Is it done?" he asked.

"Just about," J.J. replied. "The governor's son did it, without a doubt. But I need you to phone somebody to nail it down for us."

Abadie and Voire were gawking at him. Out of perversity,

he lowered his voice so that they couldn't hear the request he made of his boss.

When he replaced the phone on its cradle, Abadie said, "If you're serious, Lejern, maybe Voire should go out there and keep an eye on things."

"Not just yet. Lacombe's not going anywhere. If nobody makes him nervous, we'll have him for at least a half-hour of questions before his lawyer will arrive to shut him down."

"What the hell, though, Lejern. How do you know he did it?"

"I'll take you through it while we wait for the D.A.'s call-back," J.J. said. "Let's start with the murder scene. The single open drawer in Kim Lacombe's chifforobe. It's the one that contained the scissors. Your Mardi Gras Burglar wouldn't have known that."

"Why couldn't it have been like I thought—the Burglar searchin' the drawers?"

"There's an expensive watch on top of a table," J.J. said. "Would the Burglar have passed that by to go rooting through drawers that'd probably be full of clothes?"

"So you're sayin' Lacombe went up there, found the scissors and used 'em on his wife?" Voire asked. "Why?"

"I'll get to the motive in a minute. First, Lacombe didn't go for the scissors. His wife did. Like Dr. Macaluso said, she'd been beaten. Lacombe was pounding on her and she went for the scissors to use on him. Only her husband got them away from her and he used them instead."

"All that blood," Abadie said. "Lacombe's pretty clean."

"Yeah. Neatness counts with that lad," J.J. said. "Neatness and fashion, as we've been told. Remember his closet? What the heck were those two empty hangers doing there, with all that neatness?"

"You put something on, you leave an empty hanger," Abadie said.

"Exactly. One empty hanger was for the jacket he was wearing earlier tonight, the one that probably has his wife's blood on it. He didn't have time to get rid of it, not with smashing the window to make it look like a break-in. All he could do was stuff the bloody coat somewhere and grab a clean jacket from the closet. He was in such a hurry that he wound up with a brown coat that doesn't go so well with his blue pants. I don't suppose you'll have to search too hard to find the bloody coat. And there must be at least one person out there, maybe the maid, who isn't so self-centered they'll remember Edmund was wearing a different jacket at dinner."

"Suppos'n it went down that way, why'd he do it, Lejern?"

"Edmund told us he and his wife were keeping her pregnancy secret from Mrs. Lacombe. But he's a mother's boy. Kim knew that. The only way she got him to the altar was that mom was a couple of continents away. She'd have to know he couldn't keep a secret from the old lady."

"But he kept buttoned up," Voire said. "It was the doc who spilled the beans."

"That he did," J.J. agreed. "It wasn't only Mrs. Lacombe who was surprised. It was news to Edmund, too."

"You sayin' th' guy don't even know he'd knocked up his wife?" Voire asked.

"Well, that's the heart of the matter," J.J. said. "I think somebody did that for him and it made him mad enough to confront his wife, slap her around. That escalated into murder.

"Not that it matters, but if I were to guess who the father was, my money'd be on Paul Crain. I'm cynical enough to suspect he and the late Kim Lacombe had been lovers back in South Vietnam. Hell, they could even have plotted out her marriage to Lacombe."

"Ouch," Voire said with a wince. "I mighta killed her myself."

"This is a ver' innerestin' tale, Lejern, but I still don't see why Lacombe would be so sure he wasn't the one put the bun in the oven."

"That *is* the question and—." J.J. was interrupted by the trilling of the phone.

It was the district attorney.

J.J. listened for a minute or two, then replaced the phone.

"Well?" the police lieutenant asked.

"The D.A. had to put pressure on Edmund Lacombe's doctor, Charles Didier, but he came up with the goods."

"His doctor?" Abadie asked, heavy on the sarcasm. Then, thinking about it, he added almost apologetically, "Oh. I get what you're sayin'."

"Exactly," J.J. said. "Thanks to that run-in with the explosive in 'Nam, being a father was one thing Edmund Lacombe definitely couldn't swing."

A Murder of Import

On one of the hottest mornings of the very hot and humid New Orleans summer of 1967, J.J. Legendre was having coffee on the balcony of his French Quarter apartment when the phone rang. It was his boss, Jim Garrison. The city's district attorney.

"Sorry to bother you on your day off, Legendre," came the familiar voice from the well, "but somebody killed Andrew Fontenot last night. I don't imagine I have to tell you why I'm especially interested?"

"No, sir," J.J. replied. Fontenot, president of one of New Orleans' busiest import-export companies, had, two years before, assisted the district attorney in capturing and convicting a major drug dealer named Timmy Plata. Plata, assuming that all men of wealth were businessmen first and moralists second, had floated the suggestion to Fontenot that the importing of heroin and cocaine might just be a bit more profitable than coffee and bananas. Fontenot had gone immediately to the district attorney, who constructed a clever scheme to send Plata to Angola, one of the country's least pleasant prisons.

"Andrew Fontenot put a feather in my cap when I needed it," Garrison said. "I want whoever did this to pay hard."

"I assume Plata is still breaking rock," J.J. said.

"For the next 15 years," the district attorney assured him. "So you can scratch him off your list. That leaves you with only a million or so suspects in the Greater New Orleans area."

"Where'd the murder happen?"

"In Fontenot's office. Your pal, Lt. Abadie, is already there, probably stepping on evidence as we speak."

"I'm gone," J.J. said.

The Fontenot Building was on Royal Street, no more than seven blocks from Legendre's apartment. It was a three-story brick and concrete edifice, created by the dead man's great-grandfather, a genial robber baron who'd made millions trading with points south. Fontenot's suite of offices was on the third floor, which is where J.J. found Lt. Abadie talking with Dr. Macaluso of the coroner's office.

The police lieutenant was about as happy to see J.J. as an errant child would be to see a stern parent. "Jeeze, Lejern," he whined in his Irish Channel-Brooklyn accent, "don't you have enough to do with them Mafia killin's, you gotta stick your nose in a simple murder like this?"

"How simple is it?"

Abadie called, "Officer Bordelon!" and a young man in plainclothes stepped forward from the collection of uniformed cops and technicians. "This is Detective Lejern from the D.A.'s office. You deal with him, huh? I gotta get back to the stiff's family."

"Where's Voire?" J.J. asked, looking around for Abadie's usual partner.

"On sick leave," Abadie said as he made his exit.

Officer Bordelon smiled and said, "Voire was tryin' to kill a rat in his backyard and shot himself in the foot. Wounded in the line of duty."

J.J. stared at the young man and saw a wry grin that suggested the NOPD might finally have hired for brains. "Okay, officer, give me the run-down."

Bordelon did it without having to consult his notepad. "At approximately 10 P.M. last night—give or take an hour—a person or persons unknown entered the private office of Andrew G. Fontenot and cracked his skull with a bronze statue. It took two blows. To the back of the head and to the side of the head. There wasn't much of a struggle, which suggests that Fontenot was surprised by the attack and subdued without a fight."

"Someone he knew," J.J. said.

"Knew and trusted," Officer Bordelon said. "Like a member of his family, maybe."

"Why don't you show me the murder scene," J.J. said.

Even with police lab technicians puttering about, the room had the comfortable look of a large den. Dark green walls, decorated by framed photographs of the ships that for over a century had transported Fontenot produce. Highly polished light wood cabinets containing books and objets d'art. Thick, pale green carpet. Soft leather furniture.

An ancient cast iron safe was in one corner of the room, its open door exposing scattered envelopes and papers. An antique desk rested several feet from a window, positioned so that anyone seated at it would be facing the door, his back to the window and its view of tugboats slogging through the muddy Mississippi.

Andrew Fontenot's small, thin body was sprawled on the carpet between his desk and the chair on which he'd been seated when attacked. Blood from the wound at the side of his head had filled one of his eye sockets. His mouth was open, as if he were about to scream. Rigor was in progress. J.J. was happy the building's air conditioner was on full force.

He glanced at the bronze paperweight, in the shape of a bunch of bananas, that had been used to crack the man's skull. It was big enough to do the damage but not so large as to suggest the strength of the person wielding it. "Wiped clean," Bordelon said, reading his thoughts.

"Anything missing from the safe?" J.J. asked.

"You'll have to ask the lieutenant," Bordelon replied. "I wasn't there when he was doin' the interviewin'."

"Lead me to him."

A stenographer was just leaving as they entered what was apparently the boardroom of Fontenot Imports. Abadie was there with four other people, standing beside a handsome oak oval table. He paused and introduced J.J. to them in an awkward, hesitant manner. The attractive brunette, with a lovely though appropriately saddened face and the softest brown eyes J.J. could recall, turned out to be Louise Silver, Fontenot's private secretary. Abadie noted that she had discovered the body that morning when she arrived at the office.

The broad-shouldered young man, who resembled a well-groomed weightlifter, was Andrew Fontenot, Jr., son of the deceased, a senior at Tulane University. The pale blonde, fluttery woman in the dark dress who was dabbing at her red-rimmed eyes with a dainty kerchief was Marie Claire Fontenot, his widowed mother. That left the small, trim man in the charcoal pinstripe suit, whose angry countenance bore a remarkable similarity to the deceased: Harold Fontenot, his younger brother.

"If you're through with your inane questions, lieutenant," Harold Fontenot said to Abadie, "there are things I must be doing. Arranging for the funeral. Notifying friends and, God knows, calming down customers. I have to get back to my office and start making calls before the damned papers spread the news all over hell and gone."

"I'm finished, suh, but Detective Lejern might have a couple of questions of his own."

"Oh, my God," Harold Fontenot moaned. "I don't have time for this." He turned to J.J. "Can't you just read his notes?"

Abadie grinned at J.J. "Good question."

J.J. stared at him. "You find out what the deceased was doing here so late last night?"

Abadie's grin vanished.

"He was working," the dead man's son replied. "Dad spent most of his life here. Maybe if he'd come home with us . . ."

"Come with you?" J.J. asked. "You were here last night?"

"I was here at about six," Andrew Fontenot, Jr., said. "We all were."

J.J. looked at Abadie, who seemed surprised by the admission. "Any particular reason?" J.J. asked.

"This is a family-owned corporation," Harold Fontenot said. "Marie Claire and young Andy are both voting members."

"So you were here to vote on something?" J.J. asked.

Andrew, Jr., looked at his uncle and said nothing.

J.J. looked at the uncle, too, expectantly. "Is there a problem?" he asked.

"No. No problem," Harold Fontenot replied waspishly. "My brother and I had . . . a slight disagreement."

"Considerably more than that," the widow Fontenot said.

"Now, Marie Claire, you know that—"

"I know that you and Andy almost came to blows," she said coldly, her eyes no longer tearing.

"It was . . . business," Harold Fontenot replied with a shrug.

"What kinda business?" Lt. Abadie asked.

Harold Fontenot hesitated before replying. His nephew didn't. "The kind of business dad didn't want."

"I'm a li'l slow," the lieutenant said, annoyed that none of this had come out during his interrogation. "What kinda business would that be, egg-zackly?"

Harold Fontenot glared at the lieutenant and said nothing. The widow said, "My husband was scrupulously honest. He . . . disapproved of one of Harold's negotiations."

"There's nothing at all wrong with the deal. It's just that . . . it doesn't matter, we all agreed not to pursue it. Tomorrow, we return . . ." He paused and the color left his face. "My God, the bonds!"

He headed toward the door, but officer Bordelon blocked the way. "The bonds," Harold Fontenot gasped and tried to push past him. Bordelon held fast.

Abadie said, "Might as well let him go, son. See what's what."

They all followed Harold Fontenot back to the crime scene. The importer fell on his knees before the safe. He reached out a hand and Abadie cautioned him. "Don't touch nothin', Mr. Fontenot. The lab guys tell me the safe's been wiped clean, but still . . ."

Fontenot stared at the open safe and cried out, "They're gone!"

The inside of the safe looked like a goat's nest to J.J. Envelopes had been torn open. An assortment of twenties, fifties and hundred dollar bills were scattered, along with documents and what appeared to be stapled contracts. "Some bonds missing?" J.J. asked.

Andy Fontenot nodded vigorously. "Worth one hundred thousand dollars. Payable to bearer."

J.J. made a sound like "hmmm" and turned to find the secretary, Louise Silver, staring at him appraisingly. Her beauty was almost enough to make him forget why he was there. "You certain they're gone?" he asked.

"They were in that envelope," Harold Fontenot said, pointing to one of what seemed like four identical manila envelopes, all torn open. "I know because Marie Claire spilled some of her coffee on the corner. See?"

He pointed to a stain at the corner of the empty envelope.

"The thief didn't take the money," Officer Bordelon said, pointing to the scattered cash. "He just wanted the bonds."

"Who knew about them bonds?" Abadie asked.

"All of us," Mrs. Fontenot said. "Except Louise, of course."

"Mr. Fontenot said he wouldn't need me at the meeting at six with his family," Louise Silver said. "Which was fine, because I had a dentist's appointment at five-thirty."

"He said nothing to you about the bonds."

"No."

J.J. turned to Harold Fontenot. "Who called the meeting?"

"I did," Harold Fontenot replied. "The deal was large enough to require a vote of the members of the board."

"Then your brother knew about the bonds earlier that day?"

"No, he didn't. Andrew was an extremely conservative man. I didn't want him closing his mind before I could plead my case in person."

"Maybe you'd better tell us exactly what this deal was," J.J. said.

Harold Fontenot took a deep breath and let it out. He stared at the carpet as if he hoped it might fly him away from there. Young Andy Fontenot said, "My uncle wanted us to go into business with Fidel Castro."

"Damn it, it wasn't like that at all," Harold Fontenot said. "I'm not a crook. I know full well of the embargo against trade with Cuba. The deal I made was for shipments of rice and corn to the Caymans."

"Dad said that was a crock. Ninety percent of that shipment would wind up on Castro's table," Andy Fontenot shouted vehemently. "That's why you insisted on payments being made by bearer bonds."

"The bonds were Mr. Cardoza's idea," Harold Fontenot said.

"Who the heck is Cardoza?" Lt. Abadie wanted to know. He was informed that Emile Cardoza was the representative from the Cayman Islands who had arranged for the shipment. He had delivered the bearer bonds to Harold Fontenot the previous day, several hours before the family meeting, assuming that the deal was a fait accompli.

"Maybe we should get him in here," J.J. said.

"He's staying at the St. Charles," Harold Fontenot said, "but I don't understand what he has to do with my brother's murder. They didn't even meet."

"We'll never know," J.J. said, "unless we talk with the gent."

But, when Bordelon returned to the room ten minutes later, he reported that Cardoza had checked out of the hotel. The officer then called the Cayman Island number that Cardoza had given Harold Fontenot and it belonged to a hotel. The manager had no knowledge whatsoever of Mr. Emile Cardoza.

"That's impossible," Harold Fontenot sputtered. "He had credentials, identification, documents. He turned over one hundred thousand dollars worth of bearer bonds . . ."

J.J. stared at the apparently perplexed importer for a second or two, then surveyed the others in the room. "Well, lieutenant," he said to Abadie, "ready to make your arrest?"

"Arrest?" Abadie squawked. "Arrest who?"

J.J. was not surprised to see that Officer Bordelon had positioned himself behind the guilty party.

"The killer had the combination to the safe," J.J. told Lt. Abadie.

"How do you know that Fontenot hadn't opened it hisself?"

"Because somebody wiped the safe clean," J.J. said, then added sarcastically, "I doubt that Fontenot would have bothered."

"So where does that leave us?" Abadie asked. "All of these folks probably know the combination."

"But three of them knew that the envelope with the bearer bonds had a coffee stain on it. Which means they would not have had to tear open the other envelopes to find the bonds. That leaves us, I'm sorry to say, with Miss Silver."

Abadie was confused. "I thought we proved she didn't know about the bonds."

"Fontenot wasn't killed for the bonds," J.J. said. "This was a revenge murder, set up by the drug dealer Jimmy Plata. It was probably one of his associates who played the role of Cardoza. Miss Silver is, what, Plata's wife, daughter?"

The secretary glared at J.J., her brown eyes as hard as marble. "Sister," she said.

"Man oh man, Lejern," Abadie said, "how the hell did you make that connection?"

J.J. opened his mouth to answer, but noticed that Officer Bergeron had a wide grin on his face. "You want to respond to that?" he asked the young policeman.

Bergeron nodded. "It's easy if you've ever gone bargain huntin' in Mexico," he said. " 'Plata' is Spanish for 'silver.' "

Mad Dog

The guy who said April was the cruelest month must not have spent much time alone in Hollywood during the Christmas season. There's all that smog-filtered sun shining down. Neon trees. Elves with tans. Reindeer with chrome sidewalls. And the street decorations are flat-out cheesy—sprigs of wilted holly with greetings that are so busy being nondenominational they might as well be serving some other purpose, like telling you to keep off the grass. If there was any grass.

As you might guess from the foregoing, I was fairly depressed that night before Christmas Eve. My few friends were scattered to the winds and the holidays loomed so bleak that I was at the end of my tether. So I agreed to appear on The Mad Dog Show.

Mad Dog, last name unknown if it wasn't "Dog," was the latest thing in radio talk hosts. He was rumored to be young, irreverent, glib to the max, and funny on occasion, usually at the expense of someone else. As I discovered by listening to his show the night before my scheduled appearance, he was also brash and self-opinionated and he had an annoying habit of pausing from time to time to let loose with a baying noise. But his coast-to-coast audience was not only charmed by such behavior, it was large and loyal. And, as my publisher's publicity agent informed me, Mad Dog actually read books and was able to sell them.

Even stranger, much to the agent's surprise, the self-described "howling hound of America's airways" specifically requested that I appear on his pre-Christmas Eve show to talk about my latest novel.

His station, KPLA-FM, was in a no-man's-land just off the San Diego freeway, nestled between a large lumberyard, apparently closed for the holidays, and a bland apartment complex that looked newer than the suit I was wearing, if not more substantial. The station would have resembled a little white clapboard cottage except for the rooftop antenna that went up for nearly three stories. It was situated in the middle of a shell-coated compound surrounded by a chain fence.

Security was a big thing at KPLA-FM, apparently. A lighted metal gate blocked the only road in that I could find. I aimed my car at it, braked, and waited for a little watchman camera to spin on its axis until its lens was pointed at my windshield.

"Hello," an electronically neutered voice said, "have you an appointment?"

"I'm Leo Bloodworth," I replied, sticking my head out of the side window. "I'm guesting on the—"

"Of course," the voice interrupted me. "Mad Dog's expecting you. Please enter and park in the visitor section."

There weren't many cars. I pulled in between a black sedan and a sports convertible, got out without dinging either, and strolled to the brightly lit front door, my current novel under my arm.

The door was locked.

I couldn't find a bell, so I knocked.

A little peephole broke the surface of the door, through which an interior light glowed. A shadow covered the light and the door was opened by a pleasant woman in her senior years, rather plump and motherly. There was something familiar about her intelligent, cobalt blue eyes. Had she been an actress on one of those TV shows my family used to watch?

Aunt Somebody who was always baking cookies and dispensing comfort and advice?

"I'm Sylvia Redfern, the assistant station manager," she said. "I'm not usually here this late, but we're very short-staffed because of the holidays. Come, I'll show you to what passes for our greenroom."

She led me to a small, pale blue and white, windowless space furnished with thrift-sale sofas and chairs, a large soft-drink machine, and a loudspeaker against a far wall, from which emanated music that sounded vaguely classical.

There were two people in the room. The man was a reedy type whose lined face and sparse white hair made me place his age as somewhere in his mid-sixties, at least a decade older than me. The woman, tall and handsome with good cheekbones and short black hair, I figured for being at least twenty years my junior.

"Another fellow guest," Sylvia Redfern announced cheerily. "Ms. Landy Thorp and Dr. Eldon Varney, this is Officer Leo Bloodworth."

"Just Leo Bloodworth," I corrected, nodding to them both.

Sylvia Redfern looked chagrined. "Oh, my," she said, "I thought you were with the police."

"Not for twenty years or so. I hope our host isn't expecting me . . ."

"I'm sure his information is more up to date than mine," she replied, embarrassed. "Please make yourself comfortable. I'd better go back front and see to the other guests when they arrive."

Dr. Varney's tired eyes took in the jacket of my book. He gave me a brief, condescending smile and returned to his chair. Landy Thorp said, "You're the one who writes with that little girl."

It was true. Through a series of circumstances too painful to discuss, my writing career had been linked to that of a bright and difficult teenager named Serendipity Dahlquist. Two moderately successful books, *Sleeping Dog* and *Laughing Dog*, had carried both our names. This was the newest in the series, *Devil Dog*.

"May I?" Landy Thorp asked and I handed her the novel.

She looked at the back cover where Serendipity and I were posed in my office. "She's darling," Landy Thorp said. "Is she going to be on the show, too?"

"No. She's in New England with her grandmother." And having a real Christmas, I thought. "So I'm here solo to flog the book. What brings you to The Mad Dog Show, Miss Thorp?"

She frowned and returned *Devil Dog* as she replied, "I'm not sure I know." Then the frown disappeared and she added, "But please call me Landy."

"Landy and Leo it will be," I said. "You don't know why you're here?"

"Somebody from the show called the magazine where I work and asked for them to send a representative and here I am."

"What magazine?" I asked.

"*Los Angeles Today.*"

"*Los Angeles Today?*" Dr. Varney asked with a sneer twisting his wrinkled face. "That monument to shoddy journalism?"

Landy stared at him.

"The magazine ruffle your feathers, Doc?" I asked.

"I gather they're in the midst of interring some very old bones better left undisturbed."

Landy shrugged. "Beats me," she said. "I've only been there for a year. What's the story?"

"Nothing I care to discuss," Dr. Varney said. "Which is precisely what I told the research person who phoned me."

I strolled to the drink machine and was studying its complex instructions when the background music was replaced by an unmistakable "Ahoooooooo, ruff-ruff, ahoooooooooo. It's near the nine o'clock hour and this is your pal, Mad Dog, inviting you to step into the doghouse with my special guest, businessman Gabriel Warren. Mr. Warren has currently curtailed his activities as CEO of Altadine Industries, to head up Project Rebuild, a task force that hopes to revitalize business in the riot-torn South Central area of our city. With him are his associates in the project, Norman Daken, a member of the board at Altadine and Charles 'Red' Rafferty, formerly a commander in the LAPD, ahooooo, ahooooo, and now Altadine's head of security.

"Also taking part in tonight's discussion are Victor Newgate of the legal firm of Axminster and Newgate, mystery novelist slash private detective, Leo Bloodworth, journalist Landy Thorp, and Dr. Clayton Varney, shrink to the stars."

Varney scowled at his billing. I was doing a little scowling, myself. Red Rafferty had been the guy who'd asked for and accepted my badge and gun when I was booted off the LAPD. I suppose he'd had reason. It all took place back in the Vietnam days. Two kids had broken into a branch of the Golden Pacific Bank one night as a protest. The manager had been there and tried to shoot them and me and so I wound up subduing him and letting the kids go. The banker pushed it and Rafferty did what he thought he had to. But I never exactly loved him for it. And I was not pleased at the prospect of spending an hour with him in the doghouse.

A commercial for a holiday bloodbath movie resonated from the speaker. Dr. Varney stood suddenly and headed for the door. Before he got there, it was opened by a meek little guy carrying a clipboard. He looked like he could still be in college, with his blond crew cut and glasses. "Hi," he said, "I'm Mad Dog's engineer, Greg. This way to the studio."

"First, I demand a clarification," Dr. Varney told him: "I want to know precisely what we're going to be discussing tonight."

Greg seemed a bit taken aback by the doctor. He blinked and consulted his clipboard. "Crime in the inner city. What's causing the current rash of bank robberies. The working of the criminal mind. Like that."

"Contemporary issues," Dr. Varney said.

"Oh, absolutely," Greg replied. "Mad Dog's a very happening-now dude."

Somewhat mollified, Dr. Varney dragged along behind us as the little guy led us down a short hall and into a low-ceilinged, egg-carton-lined, claustrophobic studio with one large picture window that looked in on an even smaller control room with two empty chairs facing a soundboard.

The men seated at an oval table in the studio looked up at us. They occupied five of the nine chairs. On the table in front of each chair was a microphone. Mad Dog stood to welcome us. He was a heavyset young guy, with a faceful of bushy black beard that looked fake, and a headful of long black hair that didn't, a forelock of which nearly covered one of his baby blues. He was in shirtsleeves and black slacks and he waved us to the empty seats with a wide, hairy grin.

Since I was locking eyes with Red Rafferty while I located a chair across from him, I didn't spot the animal until I was seated. It was a weird-looking mutt nestled on a dirty, brown cushion in a far corner.

"That's Dougie Dog, the show's mascot, Mr. Bloodworth," Mad Dog explained. "We use him for the Wet

Veggie spots. He's not very active. Kinda O-L-D. But we love him."

"Is this for him?" I asked, indicating the empty chair next to me.

"No," Mad Dog smiled and settled into his chair. "The D-Dog prefers his cushion. That's for . . . someone falling by later."

"Sir?" Dr. Varney, who was hovering beside the table, addressed our host.

"Please, Doctor. It's Mad Dog."

"Mad Dog, then." Dr. Varney's lips curled on the nickname as if he'd bitten into a bad plum. "Before I participate in tonight's program, I want your assurances that we will be discussing issues of current concern."

"Tonight's topic is crime, Doctor. As current as today's newspaper. Or, in Ms. Thorp's case, today's magazine."

"Sit here, Clayton," the dapper, fifty-something Gabriel Warren said, pulling out a chair next to him for the doctor. "Good seeing you again." He looked like the complete CEO with his hand-tailored pinstripe, his no-nonsense hundred-dollar razor cut, his gleaming white shirt, and red-striped power tie. His voice was clear and confident, just the sort of voice you need if you're planning on running for the Senate in the near future, which everyone seemed to think he was. "You know Norman, don't you?" he asked Varney.

"Of course." The doc nodded to the plump, middle-aged man in a rumpled tweed suit at Warren's left hand, Norman Daken.

"What are you doin' here, Bloodworth?" my old chief asked unpleasantly. Never a thin man, he'd added about six inches around the middle and one more chin, bringing his total to three.

"Pushing my novel." I pointed to the book on the table.

He glanced at it. "Beats workin', I guess," he said.

"It takes a little more effort than having somebody stick a fifty dollar bill in your pocket," I said. That brought a nice shade of purple to his face. There'd been rumors that he'd made considerably more money as a cop than had been in his bimonthly paycheck, especially in his early days.

"Aaoooo, aaoooo," Mad Dog bayed. "Gentlemen, lady, I think Greg would like to get levels on all of us."

While each of us, in turn, babbled nonsense into our respective mikes to Greg's satisfaction, the woman who'd greeted me at the door, Sylvia Redfern, entered the engineer's cubicle and positioned the chair beside him—the better to observe us through the window.

Mad Dog asked innocently, "Any questions before we start? We've got one minute."

There was something about his manner, the edge to his voice, that made me wonder if we weren't going to be in for a few surprises before the show was over. The empty chair at our table was added intimidation. I think the feeling was shared by the others. They asked no questions, but they looked edgy, even lawyer Newgate whom I had observed in the past staying as cool as a polar bear under tremendous courtroom pressure.

Seated at his console behind the glass window, Greg stared at the clock on the wall and raised his hand, the index finger pointed out like the barrel of a gun. Then he aimed it at Mad Dog, who emitted one of his loud trademark moans. As it faded out, Greg faded in the show's theme (a rather regal-sounding melody that Landy later identified for me as Noel Coward's "Mad Dogs and Englishmen").

Then our host was telling his radio audience that they were in for a special show, one that people would be talking about through the holiday season.

Dr. Varney's frown deepened and even the smooth Gabriel Warren seemed peeved as Mad Dog blithely continued his opening comments. "Thirty years ago tonight, before I was even a little Mad Puppy, a terrible crime was committed in this city." Gabriel Warren leaned back in his chair. Norman Daken edged forward in his. Rafferty scowled. "Two crimes, really," Mad Dog corrected. "But the one people know about was the lesser of the two. The one people know about concerned the grisly death of a man of importance in this city, Theodore Daken, the father of one of our guests tonight."

Norman Daken's face turned white and his mouth dropped open in surprise. He had a red birthmark on his right cheek the size and shape of a teardrop and it seemed to glow from the sudden tension in his body. Mad Dog rolled right along. "Theodore Daken was then president of Altadine Industries, which in the early 1960s had developed one of this country's first successful experimental communications satellites, Altastar."

"Excuse me," Gabriel Warren interjected sharply. "I understood we were here to discuss urban violence."

"If Theodore Daken's death doesn't qualify," our host replied, "then I don't know the meaning of 'urban violence.' "

"Please," Norman Daken said shakily. "I don't really feel I want . . ."

"Bear with me, Mr. Daken. I'm just trying to acquaint the listeners with the events surrounding that evening. Both you and Mr. Warren were young executives at Altadine at the time, weren't you?"

"Yes, but . . ."

"You were the company's treasurer and Mr. Warren was executive vice president, sort of your father's protégé. Is that right?"

"I suppose so." The birthmark looked like a drop of blood. "I handled the books and Dad was grooming Gabe to assume major responsibilities."

"Yes," Mad Dog said. His blue eyes danced merrily. "Anyway, on that night you two and other executives—and their secretaries, that's what they called 'em then, not assistants—had your own little holiday party in a large suite at the Hotel Brentwood. A good party, Mr. Warren?"

"As a matter of fact, Norman and I both had to leave early. Theo, Mr. Daken, was expecting an important telex from overseas that needed an immediate reply. It concerned an acquisition that we knew would involve a rather sizable investment on our part and Norman was there to advise me how far we could extend ourselves."

"And you didn't return to the party?" Mad Dog asked.

"The telex didn't arrive until rather late," Warren said. "I assumed the party must have ended."

"Not quite," Mad Dog said. "You missed what sounded like, for the most part, a very jolly affair. Lots of food and drink. Altastar had gone into space and it had taken your company's stock with it. Each guest at the party was presented with a commemorative Christmas present—a model of the satellite and a hefty bonus check. And everyone was happy.

"Daken, very much in the spirit of things, presented the gifts wearing a Santa Claus suit. He didn't need a pillow. He was a man of appetite. For food and for women."

"Please," Norman Daken said, "this is so unnecessary."

"Forgive me if I seem insensitive," Mad Dog said. "But it *was* thirty years ago."

"And he *was* my father," Norman Daken countered.

"True," Mad Dog acknowledged. "I apologize. But the fact is that he did set his sights on one of the ladies that night.

184

Isn't that true, Mr. Newgate?"

"I'm not sure what point you're trying to make," lawyer Newgate said.

"Simple enough," Mad Dog replied. "On that night of nights, after all the food had been consumed, the booze drunk, and the presents dispersed, everyone left the party. Except for Daken and his new office manager. While they were alone together . . . something happened. Perhaps you can enlighten us on that, Mr. Rafferty."

Red Rafferty was living up to his nickname. He looked apoplectic. "Sure. What happened is that the woman went crazy and bashed . . . did away with poor Mr. Daken. Then she dragged his body down to her car and tried to get rid of it in a Dumpster off Wilshire."

Mad Dog's lips formed a thin line as he said, "The woman's name was Victoria Douglas and because the story about her and Theodore Daken was all anybody talked about that holiday season, she became known as 'The Woman Who Killed Christmas.' She was put on trial, found guilty by reason of insanity and sent to a hospital for the criminally insane. And, after a while, she escaped.

"She was at large for several years. Then fate caught up with her and she was discovered driving her car on an Arizona road, tripped up by a faulty brake light. She was put back into another facility and again she escaped. Five times over the past three decades did Victoria Douglas escape. She was found and brought back four times. And yes, my math is correct. The last time she escaped from a hospital, eleven years ago, she remained free.

"But The Woman Who Killed Christmas has never been forgotten. Even now, thirty years after the fact, her 'crime' remains one of the most infamous in this nation's history. And, all of you dog lovers out in radioland, here's something to chew on during the next commercial: It's entirely possible that the worst crime that took place that night wasn't the one committed by Victoria Douglas. Of that greater crime, she was the helpless victim."

Mad Dog leaned back in his chair, let loose a howl, and surrendered the airways to a commercial for soybean turkey stuffing.

Gabriel Warren stood up and turned to his associates. "Our host seems to have made a mistake inviting us here tonight. I suggest we leave him to contemplate it."

Red Rafferty knocked over his chair in his hurry to stand. Victor Newgate was a bit smoother, but no less anxious. The same was true of Dr. Varney. Norman Daken stood also. He said to Mad Dog, "I can't imagine why you're doing this terrible thing."

"How can you call it 'terrible' until you know what I'm doing?" Mad Dog asked. He turned to me. "You going, too, Bloodworth?"

"To tell the truth, I never was certain justice triumphed in the Daken case," I said. "I'll stick around to hear what's on your mind."

"Good," he said.

Since he didn't bother to ask Landy if she was staying, I figured she was in on his game, whatever it was.

The others were having trouble with the door, which wouldn't budge. Warren was losing his composure. "Open this goddamn door, son, if you know what's good for you."

"You'll be free to leave when the show is over in a little under an hour," Mad Dog informed them. "In twenty seconds we'll be back on the air. Whatever you have to say to me will be heard by nearly three million listeners. They love controversy. So feel free to voice whatever's on your mind. It can only boost my ratings."

Red Rafferty lifted his foot and smashed it against the door where the lock went into the clasp. The door didn't give and Rafferty grabbed his hip with a groan of pain.

"Not as easy as they make it seem in the police manuals, is it, Rafferty?" I asked.

"You son—" Rafferty began.

He was cut off by Mad Dog's howl. "We're back in the doghouse where some of my guests are milling about. Something on your minds, gentlemen?"

The others looked to Warren for guidance. He glared at Mad Dog and slowly walked back to his seat. The others followed. In the engineer's booth, Sylvia Redfern was viewing the proceedings with a rather startled expression on her face. In truth, I was a little startled myself at the way Mad Dog was carrying on.

"O.K., Mr. Bloodworth," he said, "why don't you tell us what you know about the night of Christmas Eve, three decades ago?"

"Why not?" And I dug into my memory bank. "I was barely in my twenties, the new cop on the beat in West L.A. My partner, John Gilfoyle, and I were cruising down Santa Monica Boulevard when we got a Code Two—that's urgent response, no siren or light. Somebody had reported a woman in distress in an alley off Wilshire.

"We arrived on the scene within minutes and found a tan Ford sedan parked in the alley with its engine going. The subject of the call was moving slowly down the alley, away from the car, a small woman in her mid to late thirties. She was in a dazed condition with abrasions on her face and arms. Her party dress was rumpled and torn.

"She didn't seem to understand who we were at first. I thought she might have been stoned, but it was more like shock. Then she seemed to get the drift and said, 'I'm the one you want, officers. I killed Theo Daken.'

"Around that time, John Gilfoyle poked his nose into her car. He shouted something to me about a big Santa Claus dummy on the backseat. Then he took a closer look and saw the blood. He ran back to our car to call in the troops."

"Did Victoria Douglas make any effort to escape?" Mad Dog asked.

"No. She was too far out of it. I don't know how she was able to drive the car."

"Did she say anything?"

"Nothing," I answered. "I had to get her name from the identification cards in her purse."

"What happened then?"

"Gilfoyle and I were helping her to our vehicle when the newspaper guys showed up. I don't know how the heck they got there that fast. I put Miss Douglas in the back of our vehicle and helped Gilfoyle pull the photographers away from the body. But they got their pictures. And the people of Los Angeles got their dead Santa for Christmas."

Norman Daken opened his mouth, but decided against whatever he was going to say. I remembered what he was like back then, sitting in the courtroom, in obvious pain. Thinner, more hair. Women might even have found him handsome. Not now. Unlike Warren, to whom the years had been more than kind, Daken resembled an over-the-hill Pillsbury doughboy.

Mad Dog turned to Rafferty. "You took charge of the Daken case personally, Mr. Rafferty. Care to say why?"

"Because it was a . . ." he began, shouting. Then, realizing that his voice was being carried on an open radio line, he started again, considerably more constrained. "Because it was a circus. There was this crazy woman who'd used a blunt instrument on Santa Claus. Not just any Santa, but a Santa

who was an old pal of the governor's. And a damn fine man."
This last was said with a glance at Norman Daken. "My chief
wanted action. That's why I took charge."

"Even though there was this tremendous pressure, you
feel that the police did all that they could in investigating the
murder?"

"Absolutely. It was handled by the book."

"Mr. Bloodworth." Mad Dog shifted back to me. "According to an account printed at the time of Victoria
Douglas's trial, you felt that maybe the detectives on the case
had missed a few bets."

"Bloodworth was a cop on the beat," Rafferty squealed.
"His opinion is worth bupkis."

"It wasn't just my opinion," I said. "Fred Loomis, one of
the investigating officers, agreed with me."

"Fred Loomis was a soak," Rafferty growled. "That's why
he took early retirement and why he wound up eating his
Colt."

"I wouldn't know about that," I said. "All I know is what
he told me. He said that the officers sent to secure the crime
scene were greener than I was and they let reporters in before
the lab boys got there. Not only that, a hotel bellboy was collecting tips to sneak curious guests into the room.

"All the evidence—the glass statue that was the supposed
murder weapon, wiped clean of fingerprints, the dead man's
clothes, the bloody pillow—all of it was polluted by a stream
of gawkers wandering through."

"But the evidence was allowed, wasn't it?" Mad Dog
asked with the assurance of a man who'd studied the trial
transcripts. He wanted to lay it out clearly for the radio audience. When no one replied, he specified, "Mr. Newgate, you
were Miss Douglas's lawyer."

"Judge Fogle allowed the evidence," Newgate said flatly.

"I objected and was overruled. It was highly irregular. I don't know what made Fogle rule the way he did. Since he's been senile for nearly fifteen years, I don't suppose I ever will."

"What was the motive for the murder?" Mad Dog asked, like a man who already knew the answer.

Rafferty didn't mind responding. "According to our investigation, Victoria Douglas had been having an affair with Daken. We figured he broke it off that night."

"Sort of a 'Merry Christmas, Honey, Get Lost' approach?" I asked.

"Yeah. Why not? He dumped her. And then made the big mistake of falling asleep on the bed. She picked up one of those satellite statues and beaned him with it. Then she hit him a few more times to be sure and lugged him down to her car."

"Without one witness seeing her," I said.

Rafferty shook his head as if I were the biggest dufus in the world. "She took the freight elevator or the stairs. My God, Bloodworth. The suite was only on the third floor."

Mad Dog was vastly amused by our interchange. The others were expressionless. Landy Thorpe winked at me.

I realized that I probably wasn't going to be plugging my book that night. But maybe this was better. As I said, I'd never felt right about the trial. And even if nothing came of this re-examination, it was getting under Rafferty's hide.

I said, "When we found Victoria Douglas, she looked like she'd been roughed up. But that wasn't mentioned at the trial."

"You can muss yourself up pretty bad swinging a heavy statue fifteen or twenty times with all your might," Rafferty explained.

"Then there's her size. She weighed about one hundred twenty-five pounds. Daken weighed twice that. How'd she get him down the stairs?"

"Maybe she rolled him down." Rafferty's little eyes flickered toward Norman Daken, ready to apologize for his crudeness. But Daken seemed to have adopted a posture of disbelief that the discussion had anything to do with him. He stared at his microphone as if he were waiting for it to suddenly dance a jig. The fingers of his right hand idly brushed his cheek where the birthmark was.

"Anyways," Rafferty said, "crazy people sometimes have the strength of ten."

"Which brings us to you, Dr. Varney," Mad Dog announced, getting back into the act. "The defense used your testimony to legitimize its insanity plea. But was Miss Douglas truly insane?"

"That was my opinion," Dr. Varney said, huffily.

"You came to this conclusion because of tests?"

"She refused to take part in tests," Dr. Varney said.

"Then it was her answers to questions?" Mad Dog inquired.

"She wouldn't answer questions. She wouldn't talk at all, except to repeat what she'd said to the police, that she'd killed Daken."

"Then how could you form a definite conclusion?"

"My God, man! All one had to do was see pictures of the corpse. It was determined that she'd hit him at least twenty times, most of the blows after he was dead."

Norman Daken closed his eyes tight.

"Ah," Mad Dog said, not noticing Norman, or choosing to ignore him. "But suppose she'd hit him only once? One fatal blow?"

Dr. Varney frowned. "I decline to speculate on what might have been. I was faced with what really did happen."

"So now we've come to the beauty part of the story," Mad Dog said, blue eyes sparkling. "What really did happen?" He lowered his hand to the floor and snapped his fingers. The ancient cur, Dougie Dog, rose up on creaky bones and padded toward him. "But first, a word from Mad Dog's own mutt about Wet Veggies."

Mad Dog lowered the mike and Dougie Dog gave out with a very laid-back but musical bark. Greg, the engineer, followed the bark with a taped commercial for a dog food that consisted of vegetables "simmering in savory meat sauce." I was feeling a little peckish, myself.

Gabriel Warren tapped Victor Newgate on the arm and asked, "How many laws is our friend Mad Dog breaking by holding us here against our will?"

"Enough to keep him off the radio for quite a few years, I'd think," Newgate replied.

"C'mon, guys," Mad Dog told them. "Aren't you even the least bit interested in where we're headed?"

Norman Daken's eyes moved to the picture window where Greg was staring at the clock and Sylvia Redfern was looking at us with concern. His fingers continued their nervous brushing of his cheek near the birthmark. "Where are we headed?" he asked, so softly I could barely hear him.

"Thirty years ago, I would have been interested," Warren said dryly. "Today, I couldn't care less. It's old news."

Dougie Dog put his paws on his master's leg and made a little begging sound. Mad Dog reached into his jacket pocket and found a biscuit that he placed in the animal's open mouth. "Good old boy," he said.

"Family dog?" I asked.

Mad Dog smiled at me and his clear blue eyes didn't blink. "Yes," he said. "Fact is, he was given to me by my mother when I moved out on my own."

"You can sit there and talk about dogs all you want," Dr. Varney said. "But I am definitely not going to let you get by with—"

"Awoooo, awoooo," Mad Dog interrupted. "We're back again, discussing the thirty-year-old murder of industrialist Theodore Daken. You were saying, Dr. Varney?"

"Nothing, actually."

"We were getting to a description of what really happened in the murder room that night."

"What happened is public record," Rafferty said. "The verdict was in three decades ago. Case closed. Some of you guys like to play around with stuff like this, but you can't change history."

"Things do happen to make us doubt the accuracy of history books, however. Look at all the fuss over Columbus. Or the crusades. Or maybe a murder case that wasn't murder at all."

"What the devil's that mean?" Rafferty asked.

"This really is quite absurd," Gabriel Warren said flatly. "Why Victoria Douglas killed Theo Daken three decades ago is an intriguing question, but its answer will solve none of today's problems. We should be discussing the murders that take place every seven hours in this city, or the bank robberies that take place on an average of one every other day."

"That's what I thought we were here to talk about," Victor Newgate added.

"We can discuss crime in L.A. for the next year and not come up with any concrete answers," Mad Dog said. "But tonight, it's possible that we will actually be able to conclude what really happened to Theodore Daken. Isn't that worth an hour of your time?"

"You're going to solve the Daken murder?" Rafferty asked sneeringly.

"Actually, I was hoping to leave the solving to Mr. Bloodworth."

"Huh?" I replied. "Thanks for the vote of confidence,

Mad Dog. But I'm not exactly Sherlock Holmes. I'm just a guy who plods from one point to another."

"Plod away, then."

"The world turns over a few times in thirty years, and its secrets get buried deeper and deeper. Too deep to uncover in an hour."

"Suppose we make it a little easier?" Mad Dog said.

I thought I knew where he was headed. I pointed at the empty chair at the table. "If Victoria Douglas were to come out of hiding and join us, that might make it easier."

The others didn't think much of that idea. They eyed the chair suspiciously. "She's still a wanted woman," Rafferty said. "And it'd be my duty to perform a citizen's arrest and send her back where she belongs."

"Don't worry," Mad Dog said. "The chair's not for her. Is it, Miss Thorp?"

We all turned to Landy expectantly. "Victoria Douglas is dead," she stated flatly. It was the first sentence she'd spoken since we all sat down and it more than made up for her silence. "She died of a heart attack nearly six months ago in the Northern California town of Yreka, where her neighbors knew her as Violet Dunn. Knew and loved her, I should add."

The others seemed to relax. Then Landy said, "Before she died, we had many long talks together."

"What kind of talks?" Gabriel Warren asked.

"Talks that I'm using in an article on Victoria Douglas for my magazine."

Dr. Varney exclaimed, "I told you about it, Gabriel. Someone phoned my office."

"N-nobody called me," Norman Daken said.

"You're on my list," Landy told him. "We're just starting the major research. I'll be calling each of you."

Warren stared at her appraisingly. Rafferty seemed

amused. "So, honey, on these long talks you supposedly had," he asked, "did she happen to mention anything about the murder?"

Landy stared at him. "She told me that she killed Theodore Daken in self-defense. It was she who fell asleep that night. She was not used to alcohol and had had too much champagne. When she awoke, Daken was beside her on the bed in his underwear, trying to remove her clothes.

"She called out, but everyone else had gone. She tried to push him away and he slapped her across the face. Struggle seemed useless. He was a big, powerful man. Her hand found the statue somehow and she brought it down against his skull. Then she blacked out. She doesn't remember hitting him more than once."

"Doesn't remember? That's damn convenient," Rafferty said. "No wonder she didn't try that yarn on us at the time."

"She might have," Mad Dog informed us, "if she'd taken the stand at her trial."

Newgate waved a dismissive hand. "She would have hurt her case immensely. It was my feeling that, in light of the grisly aspects of the situation, she was better off with an insanity plea. She could only have hurt that defense by taking the stand."

"She told me she did mention self-defense at her first parole hearing," Landy said.

"And, alas, as I feared, they didn't believe her," Newgate said. "I suppose that's what pushed her into making her initial escape."

"How did you come to be her lawyer, Newgate?" I asked.

He stared at me as if he didn't feel he had to waste his time responding. But we were on radio, so he replied, "I'd met her socially."

"You mean you'd dated her?" I asked.

"No. But, from time to time, I had lunch with her and . . . other employees of Altadine. The firm I was working for did quite a lot of business with the company."

"Did Daken sit in on these lunches?" I asked.

"The old man? Hardly," Newgate replied with a smile. "He was the CEO. We were a few rungs down."

"Who else would be there?" Mad Dog wondered.

Newgate brushed the question away with an angry hand. "I don't really know. An assortment of people."

"Mr. Warren?" I asked.

"I was part of the crowd," Warren said. "Eager young execs and pretty women who worked for the company. Victoria Douglas included. There was nothing sinister about it. Nothing particularly significant, either."

"According to testimony from a woman named Joan Lapeer," Mad Dog said, "Miss Douglas had been Theodore Daken's girlfriend. Did she confirm that, Miss Thorp?"

"Victoria told me that Joan Lapeer had been Altadine's office manager before her. Theodore Daken fired the woman and hired Victoria. Joan Lapeer was so bitter that she spread the word that Daken had wanted to hire his girlfriend."

"Then there was no truth to it?"

"None," Landy said. "Victoria told me she'd only met Daken once or twice before she went to work for Altadine."

"Met him where?" I asked.

"Joan Lapeer was a very lazy, very incompetent worker," Gabriel Warren suddenly announced. Norman Daken looked up from the table at him, without expression.

"So she lied about Victoria Douglas's involvement with Theodore Daken," Mad Dog said.

"Miss Douglas said he asked her out a few times," Landy told us. "But she always refused."

"Because he was her boss?" Mad Dog asked. "Or a fat slob, or . . . ?"

"Because she was involved with someone else," Landy said.

"Who?"

Landy shook her head. "She wouldn't name him. She said it was the one oath she would never break."

"She used the word, 'oath'?" I asked.

"Precisely."

"Is he our mystery guest?" I asked Mad Dog, indicating the empty chair.

"No," he said, turning toward Greg in the booth. "But this might be a good time to cut to a commercial." He nodded, let out one of his wails and Greg responded to the cue with a spot announcement for a holiday lawn fertilizer, "The perfect gift for the gardener around your home."

"How much longer are you going to hold us here against our will?" Warren demanded.

"The old clock on the wall says another nineteen minutes."

"This is going to turn into a very expensive hour," Warren said.

"Why don't you just make your point," lawyer Newgate said to our host, "and be done with it? Why must we put up with this cat-and-mouse routine?"

"That's how radio works," Mad Dog replied. "We have to build to a conclusion." He leaned toward me. "Are you willing to give us a wrap-up, Mr. Bloodworth, of what you think happened that night?"

"I wouldn't want to go on record with any heavy speculation. You don't seem to care about these litigious bozos, but I personally would just as soon stay clear of courtrooms."

"No need to mention any names," he said. "Just give us . . ."

He paused, some sixth sense informing him that the commercial had ended and he was about to go back on the air. He let out a howl and said, "Welcome back to the doghouse. Private Detective Leo Bloodworth is about to give us his version of what happened back at that hotel thirty years ago."

"Well," I said. "I'll take Victoria Douglas's word for it that she acted in self-defense. That would explain her battered condition. But if the guy attacked her and she repelled him, why wouldn't she just stay there and call the cops?"

"Because she panicked?" Landy speculated.

"When you panic, you run away. But Rafferty and his detectives tell us she didn't do that. Their scenario has her hanging around the suite and finally taking the body with her when she left. Why would she do that?"

"The dame was crazy." Rafferty was almost beside himself.

I replied, "She's just killed a man. She's confused. She decides to take the dead guy with her? Nobody's that crazy. Wouldn't it have been much more natural for her to just run away? Probably down the service stairs?"

"That's your trouble, Bloodworth," Rafferty said. "You refuse to believe what your eyes tell you. You saw her with the stiff."

"That was later. What I think is that she ran away to the one person she trusted—the guy she was in love with. She told him what had happened in the hotel suite. He said he'd help her, but she had to promise to keep him out of it, no matter what.

"They went back to the hotel in her car, parking it near the service exit. Maybe they went up together. Maybe he told her to stay in the car. He, or the both of 'em got Daken's body down in the service elevator. They put it in the back of Victoria Douglas's car. By then, she was in no condition to drive. So the boyfriend drove to the alley off Wilshire. And here's where it gets a little foggy. For some reason the boyfriend ran out on her and left her to face the music all alone. And true to her promise, her 'oath,' she refused to name him. Even though it made her look like a crazy woman."

"Wait a minute, Bloodworth," Rafferty blustered. "If it didn't make sense for her to move the body, why did this imaginary boyfriend decide to do it?"

"Because there would be less scandal if Daken were found beaten to death in an alley wearing a Santa Claus suit than if he turned up dead in a hotel room in his skivvies."

"You're saying that Theodore Daken was moved to salvage his reputation?" Mad Dog asked.

"And his company's," I said. "I assume Douglas's boyfriend was an executive at Altadine."

"Why?" Mad Dog asked.

"That's one way Victoria Douglas would have met Daken once or twice before he hired her. It's also how she would have known about the job opening. Maybe the boyfriend got Daken to hire her. Anyway, he was the one who was trying to downplay any scandal."

"Only it didn't work," Mad Dog said.

"And I bet the guy next in line to the presidency, Gabriel Warren, had quite a job on his hands keeping Altadine's investors high on the company." I looked at him.

"You're right about one thing," he said. "It would have been quite a lot easier if Theo's death had been minus the sordid details. But as bad as it got, I managed."

"I'll bet you did," I said.

"Wait a minute!" Landy interrupted. "This was a company Christmas party. If Victoria's lover had been an

Altadine exec, would he have just gone off, leaving his girl-friend passed out and easy prey for Daken?"

"I think the guy left the party early, before she was in any danger," I said, looking at Warren.

"Would you care to take a guess at the name of Victoria Douglas's lover, Mr. Bloodworth?" Mad Dog asked.

I continued staring at Gabriel Warren. "Like I said, some-body who left the party early. Somebody who wanted to squelch the scandal. But when that didn't happen, he was shrewd enough to know when to cut and run. Somebody smooth and savvy and well connected enough to know how to push the right buttons to keep himself clear of the fallout."

"How would he do that?" Mad Dog asked. Warren glared at me.

"By pressuring a high-ranking police officer to disregard a few facts that didn't jibe with the official story of how Daken died. By getting a defense lawyer to plead his client insane and keep her off the stand, just to make sure his name didn't come up in testimony. By convincing a judge to bend a few rules. All to keep one of America's great corporations flying high. Because, surely, if one more guy at the top of Altadine had got caught by that tar baby, the company might never have recovered."

"You're not going to name him?" Mad Dog asked.

"He knows who he is," I said, nodding at Warren.

I was hoping to get the guy to do something. Like snarl. Or show his fangs. When he didn't, I said, "It just occurred to me that maybe Victoria Douglas didn't really kill Theodore Daken at all. She told Miss Thorp that she didn't remember hitting him more than once. Suppose that wasn't enough to do the job, though she thought it was. Suppose the boyfriend went up to that hotel room, saw Daken on the bed sleeping off that nonfatal whack and picked up the statue and finished the job, wiping the weapon clean. Then he had an even stronger reason for wanting Victoria Douglas to keep quiet about his participation in the removal of the body. What do you think, Warren?"

"You're making a big mistake," he hissed.

"That's the story of my life," I told him.

"This may be the perfect time to bring in our mystery guest," Mad Dog said. And almost at once, the door opened and a wizened old man entered. He looked like he was a hundred-and-one, his khaki pants flapping against his legs, his bright red windbreaker hanging on his bony frame. A plaid cap with a pompom covered his bald pate at a jaunty angle.

The door slammed behind him and he turned and looked at it for a second.

"We've just been joined by Mr. Samuel J. Kleinmetz," Mad Dog informed his listening audience, which included me. "Mr. Kleinmetz, would you please take this chair?"

As the old duffer shuffled to the chair, Mad Dog said, "Mr. Kleinmetz was working that night before Christmas Eve, thirty years ago. What was your occupation, sir?"

The old man was easing himself onto the chair. "Eh?"

"Occupation."

"Nothing," he said, louder than necessary, sending Greg jumping for his dials. "Been retired for fifteen years. Used to drive a cab, though. Beverly Hills Cab. Drove a Mercedes. Leather seats. Wonderful radio. Worked all the best hotels . . ."

"Good enough," Mad Dog said, stemming the man's flow. "You were working the night . . ."

"The night the woman killed Christmas?" the old man finished. "Sure. I worked six days a week, fifty-two weeks a year. I was working that night, absolutely."

"In the Wilshire district?"

"That's where I used to park and wait," the old man said. He squinted his eyes in delight, staring at the microphone. "This is working?" he asked.

"I hope it is," Mad Dog told him. "On that night, you picked up a passenger not far from where they later found the body of Theodore Daken?"

"The dead guy in the Santa Claus suit, yeah. I guess it was minutes before. The paper said they found the guy at about ten-thirty. I picked up my fare at maybe ten-twenty."

"How the devil can he remember that?" Gabriel Warren snapped. "It was thirty years ago."

"There are days you remember," the old man said. "I can remember the morning I woke up to hear the Japs bombed Pearl Harbor. I can tell you everything that happened that day. And the day that great young president John Fitzgerald Kennedy was assassinated by that Oswald creep. And the night the woman killed Christmas."

"We showed Mr. Kleinmetz photographs of the members of the executive board of Altadine taken that year," Mad Dog said. "He identified his passenger. We then showed him a photograph of that same man today. Would you tell us if he's in this room tonight?"

"Sure." Sam Kleinmetz looked across the table in the direction of Gabriel Warren, and I could feel a smug grin forming on my face. "That's him right there."

My smug grin froze. Kleinmetz was pointing a bony finger at Norman Daken. "You didn't have to show me all those pictures. He's changed a lot, but I'd have known him right away, as soon as I saw that red dot on his face. Never seen one quite like it before or since."

Daken looked more relaxed than he had all evening. "So many years ago," he said, almost wistfully. "I'd almost forgotten. As if anyone could."

"Don't say another word, Norman," Gabriel Warren cautioned.

"No more, Gabe. I don't want to hold it in any longer. My father and I . . . we had our disagreements. He thought I was weak. I suppose I am. Look what I did to the woman I loved."

In the engineer's booth, both Greg and Sylvia Redfern were totally caught up in the tableau in the studio.

"I think that's why my father felt he had to have Victoria," Norman continued. "Because I loved her. The bastard ruined it all for us. It was all his fault, not hers, poor woman. She fought him and knocked him unconscious. She didn't hate him, you see. Not like I did."

Warren was scowling at him. "What the devil are you—?"

"Bloodworth is right. I killed him, Gabe. I thought you knew that."

"You thought I . . . ? How could . . . ?" Warren was having trouble articulating.

Norman Daken gave him a pitying smile. "He wanted you to be his son, Gabe. And he got me instead."

"I would never have helped—"

"That's what was so beautiful about it. You fixed it so that I stayed clear of it."

"I was trying to save the company," Warren said. "But if I'd known . . ."

"Well, now you do," Norman Daken told him.

I said, "I always wondered why we got called to that alley that night. That was you, wasn't it, Norman? You deserted that poor woman in the alley and went off to call the cops."

"I didn't want to hurt Vicki, I swear it," he said. "I told her that she would never go to prison and I lived up to that. Thanks to Gabe's influence."

"But she wasn't exactly free," I said.

"No," Norman agreed.

"And you were."

"That depends on your definition of the word," he said.

Station KPLA-FM went off the air early that night, even though the police made short work of their task. They came, they saw, they escorted Norman off to be booked. As they explained, there was no statute of limitations on murder.

As for the crimes Gabriel Warren and his associates may have committed, the police were less certain of their footing. So that foursome left on their own recognizance. Even if it turned out to be too late to nail them for railroading Victoria Douglas into the nut house, they probably wouldn't be suing Mad Dog or myself. And I doubted I'd be seeing Warren's name on any ballots in the near future.

When they'd all departed, leaving only Mad Dog, Landy, Dougie Dog, and myself in the main studio, I asked, "Are you both her children?"

"Just me," Mad Dog admitted, grinning. "What tipped you?"

"Dougie Dog, for one," I said, looking at the drooping mongrel. "The family hound, you said. Dougie. Douglas. And then, there's your nickname. Mad Dog. Madison Douglas?"

"Nope. Just Charlie Douglas. The 'mad' is, well, they said she was mad and what happened to her made me pretty angry. My dad worked at the hospital where Mom spent her first three years. He helped her escape. When she was sent back, I was raised by my paternal grandparents."

"And you kept her name?"

"It's mine, too. They never married officially. How could they? Anyway, figuring out that I was her son, that was good detecting."

"It's the least I could do after picking the wrong murderer," I said.

"We didn't know about the murder," Landy said. "Poor Victoria always thought she'd killed Daken."

"Who are you?" I asked. "Just a friend of the family?"

"As I said, I'm a journalist. I happened to rent a house next door to Victoria's a few years ago. We became friends and eventually she opened up to me about who she was. I think she hoped Charlie and I might get together."

"And you did."

They both smiled.

The dog rose to its feet, yawning, and dragged itself to the door and out of the studio.

"And you two decided to clear Victoria's name," I said.

"Right again," Charlie "Mad Dog" Douglas said. "Thanks for the help."

I stood up and picked my book from the table. "I didn't sell many of these tonight," I said.

"Come on back," he offered.

"It's too bad your mother passed away without ever learning the truth about that night."

They both nodded solemnly.

I left them and wandered out into the corridor. A light was on in the greenroom. As I passed, I saw Sylvia Redfern sitting on the couch, reading a book. Dougie Dog was curled up at her feet, sleeping peacefully. Her eyes, blue as a lagoon, blue as Mad Dog's, suddenly looked up and caught me staring at her. She smiled.

"Goodnight, Mr. Bloodworth," she said. "Thanks for everything."

I told her it was my pleasure and wished her a very merry Christmas.

"It will be," she replied. "The merriest in years."

DATE DUE			